I0530096

Consequences Can Be Fatal

Lee Smith

Copyright © 2023 L K Smith
All rights reserved.

The characters and events portrayed in this book are fictitious. Any
similarity to real persons, living or dead, is coincidental and not intended
by the author.

No part of this book may be reproduced, or stored in a retrieval
system, or transmitted in any form or by any means, electronic,
mechanical, photocopying, recording, or otherwise, without express written
permission of the publisher.

ISBN 13: 978-0-6458674-0-4

For my lovely "first draft" readers – Alli, Carrie, Sandy and Sue – thank you for your support and encouragement.

And so it begins …

Every workplace has that "office witch".

Male, female, young, old; they make the work day a misery. A quiet bully; a loud mocker or someone who's just plain mean; they create havoc wherever they go. At some point everyone has fantasised about them being dead and gone.

This is the story of someone who actually made it happen.

And every murder mystery has to have a body …

This body was found in the office photocopier room.

The copier room was down the hall from the general office for the local council. Originally it was another smaller separate office but with all the complaints about the noise of the copier, an earlier tenant had converted the room into what it was today. People still grumbled about having to go down the hall to copy and collect their printing but it was impossible to please everyone.

The door from the hallway opened into a long skinny room with the photocopier at the far end and a bench table down the left-hand side for people to sort their papers. Under the bench was the spare toner cartridges and storage space for extra copy paper in all the different sizes. Opposite the bench was the shredder, the security bin, empty boxes piled up waiting for recycling and a chair which was often occupied by those waiting for their printing to appear.

On the day of the murder, an 'Out of Order' sign was prominently displayed on the hallway door. The overhead lights were turned off with the room eerily lit by the digital display screen of the photocopier.

Next to the photocopier was a pile of empty copy paper boxes with one foot artistically poking out.

As the boxes were cleared away, the dead body with wide unseeing eyes was revealed.

chapter one

S even days earlier …

This tale starts, like many things do, with food. It's always surprising how one decision can have such wide-reaching consequences.

Most Tuesday night's a group of old friends from St Matthew's Girls Private School get together to catch up on the past week. These friends include twins; Belle and Lucy Anderson, Jules Sullivan, Georgie Wilson and Charlotte Evans.

While some things had changed since school, many had stayed the same. Belle was still the leader; fiercely independent and career focussed, while Georgie had grown into an animal loving vegetarian, recently married and hoping for children soon. Charlie (never Charlotte) was the group's fitness freak, always training for some marathon while Jules was newly engaged and busy planning her wedding.

Even after nearly fifteen years since school, they never ran out of things to talk, laugh and argue about. Tonight's major topic was Lucy's disastrous love life.

Lucy had dated lots of men since leaving school including an accountant, a clown, a plumber and the current beach bum. Opinions within the group are divided as to why Lucy had such varied tastes and why her relationships always ended up in ruins. Some think Lucy keeps her heart safe, others just consider her a free spirit with no desire to settle down.

"Am I late?" panted Georgie as she fell into the last vacant chair, "I ran all the way from the car."

"You need more exercise," Charlie, with little tact, retorted.

"Hey, I get plenty of exercise from the dogs."

Lucy, always the peacemaker, interrupted by leaning across Charlie to hand Georgie a menu, "Choose some food, I'm starving."

This week they were having dinner at a local pub set in the Adelaide foothills surrounded by towering gum trees. It was a lovely old pub established in 1891 according to the sign in the entrance. Although the outside was antique stonework and rustic decorations, the inside had clean lines with all the modern amenities including the often disputed pokies. Drinks were reasonable but the meals were the major drawcard for locals and those from further afield. Real old fashioned pub meals that were warm, hearty and filling which bucked the current trend that valued presentation over flavour and substance.

The evening views of the nearby shrub were beautiful as always, although the area was already showing signs of the dry growth that predicted a long and dangerous bushfire season. And it was only the beginning of November! November was spring in Adelaide, where the weather was just starting to warm up for the coming summer. Days are fine, while nights are cool and there was still a chance of rain.

Adelaide was the coastal capital of South Australia and the fifth most populous city in Australia with a population of around 1.3 million people.

Adelaide was known for its wine regions such as the Barossa Valley and McClaren Vale, a fact that Belle and Lucy's parents were happy to corroborate. They had spent many an afternoon wine tasting at one of the many vineyards in the surrounding areas.

Its other claim to fame was all the festivals held in Adelaide such as The Fringe, Adelaide Film Festival, Illuminate Adelaide and many more. It was nearly impossible to find accommodation during Mad March and all of the friends had housed interstate or international visitors at some point.

After the friends ordered meals and got fresh drinks, Charlie returned to the previous conversation, "Georgie, it's up to you. What's your vote? Does Lucy stay with Kaili or not?"

As if this was a normal way to decide the outcome of a relationship, Georgie considered the question, "Who's for and who's against?"

"Belle and I are for booting the bum out and Jules sappily thinks he should be given another chance." Charlie replied.

Charlie Evans had been with the police force since leaving school and had worked her way up to Detective Senior Constable. Being a cop suited her quiet forceful personality; plus she was very health conscious and loved exercise. She'd recently broken up with her long term boyfriend and consequently had little trust in relationships.

"What's he done this time?" asked Georgie.

"Nothing!" objected Lucy.

"Unless you count borrowing $200, skipping work and taking off down to Victor for the week," mumbled Belle, "You're never going to see that money again."

Lucy and Kaili have been dating for nearly a year now with plenty of ups and downs. Kaili Shaw comes from a family that historically had not succeeded. His parents have always believed that the government owes them a living; influencing both Kaili and his two older brothers who encourage him to skip work and go surfing with them. Kaili, born David, had renamed himself with the Hawaiian name for a Hawaiian deity, and was the quintessential beach bum; tall, muscular with shaggy blonde hair and scruffy beard.

"That's not too bad," said Georgie, clearly not wanting to upset Lucy, "He might pay it back."

Belle just rolled her eyes, while Charlie snorted her contempt for this idea. It was obviously two against two with Lucy as the tiebreaker.

"So what's been happening with your future mother-in-law this week?" Lucy asked Jules, desperately trying to change the subject.

Jules Sullivan was the real beauty of the group; tall, slender with a well-shaped blonde pixie cut. After a steady stream of boyfriends, Jules had just become engaged to Andrew and her latest obsession was planning a gorgeous wedding. She loved bargain hunting for the latest fashions and was the best dressed trainer at the charity organisation where she taught office skills to the long term unemployed.

"She's getting worse," replied Jules, "The latest argument has been about the location. Drew and I want to get married at the zoo; she wants it to be at her church. She thinks Drew will cave more easily and has been ringing him at least every day with reasons why the zoo is not the right place."

"Will Drew give in?" asked Belle.

"No. He really doesn't want to get married in a church so even if she convinces him against the zoo, it's still not going to be her church."

Jules, Belle and Lucy continued to discuss the plans for the wedding while Georgie and Charlie quietly argued about Kaili.

Just as Charlie was about to return the conversation to Lucy's love life, the food was delivered and after a few moments the talk moved on to daily happenings.

"Georgie, how's Oliver's workload going? Has it calmed down since last week?"

"No. He's still working twelve hours most days. The dogs and I hardly see him. I'll be really glad when this settles."

Georgie Wilson was the classical girl next door; short, full figured with bouncy blonde curls. She was light hearted and cheerful except when it came to any form of animal cruelty - then the fangs came out. Married last year to her high school sweetheart, Oliver, they have rescued two mutts from Animal Welfare and if Georgie's not at work as a vet nurse, she's somewhere with their dogs.

"It must be the new moon," Charlie interjected, "All the loons are coming out to play. We've had so many reports of vandalism lately, especially around the schools."

"You've been busy too? We've been run off our feet with animals having accidents and ending up at the vets."

"What about you guys? It must be easier at the council now Paige is there to help? How's she fitting in?" Jules asked the twins.

Belle and Lucy looked at each other. Paige Raynor had completed her office training with Jules last year and when a vacancy came up recently at the council, Jules had suggested that she apply. Paige had gotten the job and was considered one of Jules's success stories.

"Her work is quite good," replied Lucy.

"When she actually does any," Belle was less tactful.

Paige was a party girl. With her short and skinny stature, she liked to dress well and managed this with financial help from her indulgent parents. The youngest of three kids from older parents, she had grown up in a world that caters for her every need and can't understand why this won't continue in her new working world.

Jules blushed slightly, "Well at least her work's good. Maybe she'll improve once she gets used to the place."

"And it is hard to start in a new workplace," Lucy said, "We've got so many different characters all mixed together in one small office."

Belle was the one who snorted this time. Charlie and Georgie hid smiles behind their hands while Jules quickly offered to get some more drinks.

The chatter ranged from Belle's latest favourite reality TV show to the progress of Jules's garden. Georgie piped in with her current animal cause, trying to generate more contributions, and Charlie told of her recent shooting practice. Lucy was quiet during all this noise and seemed to be lost in thought.

"I have to go. Oliver promised he'd be home by 9.00pm and it would be nice to see him while he's awake." Georgie stood up and gathered her handbag and jacket, "Same time next week? Let's try that new Asian place in Modbury? I'll make a reservation for 7.00pm?"

The rest of the group murmured agreement while starting to make going home moves too. As they left the pub and walked to the car park, Charlie edged nearer to Lucy, "So any decision about Kaili?"

"Yeah. He's got to go. You're right, he keeps taking advantage of me," Lucy said quietly, "But not a word to Belle, I hate it when she's right. I'll tell him next weekend then tackle Belle."

"Okay," Charlie smiled giving Lucy a quick one arm hug, "I'm sure it won't be as bad as you think."

As goodbyes were exchanged and they all moved towards their cars, no-one was aware of how Lucy's decision to move on was going to change their world.

chapter two

Belle and Lucy shared a small, rented house in a leafy suburb to the north east of Adelaide. Cooper, Belle's four year Rhodesian Ridgeback, lived with the twins and ruled the place from his favourite spot in front of the heater.

The house had been built on a subdivided block so it was long and skinny. Three bedrooms, two bathrooms, beige walls and virtually no backyard to maintain. It was like so many of the houses built in the last few years.

Belle had always been a leader; from being born seven minutes before her twin to being elected school captain. She was faithfully followed by Lucy who missed out on the intensity gene. As identical twins, physically there was little difference but their personalities were like night and day. Belle was career focussed, independent and driven, while Lucy was very laid back with wide ranging interests. Both work for the council but while Belle was looking for promotion, Lucy was more interested in reading tarot cards.

As she expertly parked her car under the carport, Belle looked across at her sister and asked, "Is everything okay?"

"Yeah, I'm just tired," replied Lucy, "I only need some sleep."

The twins walked inside their little home and were greeted by Cooper who had deigned to rouse himself from his bed in Belle's room.

"Want a coffee?" asked Lucy as she threw her handbag on the couch.

"No thanks, but a biscuit would be nice."

While Lucy got herself a cuppa and the biscuits, Belle turned the television on and played with Cooper.

The television was in the living room. The room was a reasonable size; square with just enough room for two small black leather couches plus television, a tall, wooden bookcase and a square coffee table in the middle of the room. The heater took up most of one wall and the rug in front was Cooper's favourite spot. The other walls showed various prints from old movies. The twins spent many hours here in the winter watching movies and reading books (or tarot cards for Lucy).

Coffee and/or biscuits in hand, they curled up on the couches, with Cooper snuggled under Belle's legs.

"What are we going to do about Arthur? We can't just let it go?"

"What can we do? It's not like we're in charge and if Jack doesn't notice or do anything, do you really want to complain to Mark?"

Both twins worked in the Animal Awareness and Control Department. Their section was responsible for ensuring owners of animals within the council areas followed the rules and that they were aware of these rules. The major focus was on dogs and included collecting dog registrations, following up barking complaints, running weekly dog training, managing multiple dog parks and conducting publicity events like the current 'Masterchef for Dogs'.

Every year the council held a Pet Expo to raise awareness of pet regulations and provide an opportunity for local businesses to advertise their pet related products. Over the last couple of years, attendance had been dropping and the department was searching for ways to fix this.

With the Masterchef television show enjoying a surge in popularity, Belle had the idea to run a similar competition for dogs.

There would be two competitions; the first to find the best home cooked dog treat and the other to have the family dog as a doggie taste tester. The doggie taste testers would be decided by a kid's colouring competition while applicants for the cooks would need to describe in one hundred words or less the history of their recipe.

Once the cooks and testers had been selected, the cook off would be the main attraction of the Pet Expo. On the actual day of the expo, there would be four rounds with eight cooks trying out their recipe each time. At the end of each round, all the treats would be tested by four different dogs. From each round, the two treats judged to be the favourites by the dogs (and a human judge) would go to the final. The last round with the best eight cooks would be the final event of the day. The winners would be decided by four more dogs and a celebrity chef; although the chef wouldn't actually be tasting the treats! The winner would receive a year's supply of dog food with monthly toys and treats and the runner ups would get a gift bag with toys and treats.

The rules for both competitions had been established with all the associated paperwork and the details had been on the council website for the last six weeks. With only email and website advertising, the number of entries they'd received was pleasing and with only a few days left before the competitions closed, the cooks and doggie taste testers would soon be decided.

In addition to the cooking competition, the expo would showcase a variety of pet related businesses. Possible exhibitors such as pet shops, pet accessories, training schools, and of course pet food suppliers had been contacted. There was even going to be a butcher available.

Then the people side of things needed to be considered like people food and drinks. It was decided to have a range of stalls available; donuts, sausage sizzle, drinks, pies/pasties, Chinese, baked potatoes plus a healthy option. And, of course, everything needed permits and approvals to be organised.

As the main organiser of the event, Belle was constantly being amazed by all the little details that needed to be handled. Today's surprises contained people entering as both cooks and tasters, cooks wanting three hours for making the treats, allergic dogs entering the taster competition and the list went on forever.

So far, a date had been agreed and the Community Park reserved; sponsors, exhibitors, vets and food stalls had been organised; the mayor had been confirmed to open the expo; plus the advertising of the expo itself had been arranged.

The major jobs still to be done were to complete the initial competitions and put together an information pack. Then naturally finishing all the half completed tasks.

It had been a massive undertaking and was proceeding full speed ahead with the pet expo scheduled in early December just before Christmas.

Like any government agency, office politics were ever present and the problem was who was doing the work and who was claiming they were.

"But Arthur is taking credit for everything you're doing with the Pet Expo and nobody is saying anything," complained Lucy.

"I have a plan," replied Belle.

"What?"

"We're having a status meeting tomorrow with Jack to check on all the jobs. If I make sure to say exactly who has done what, then Jack has to notice that Arthur really hasn't done anything, regardless of what he says."

"What if Arthur lies? Or Jack doesn't do anything?"

"Then the time for subtly is over," Belle announced dramatically and joked, "I'll punch Arthur in the nose and tell Jack it's all his fault."

Belle was disappointed in Jack. Perhaps he wasn't the man she admired. He should have noticed what was happening and made sure that Belle got the recognition that she deserved. A cute butt didn't make up for taking the easy road.

She wasn't surprised by Arthur; this wasn't the first time he'd claimed credit for someone else's work but it was the most obvious. And Kelly, the Assistant Event Coordinator, who worked with Belle and Arthur, was unfortunately too quiet to stand up for either herself or Belle.

"Yeah, I can just see you doing that. But seriously, what will you do?"

"If this doesn't work, I think it's time I actually spoke to Jack about it, Arthur has gone too far this time. It won't be nice but unless you have any other suggestions, it might be my only choice."

"I hope the meeting goes well tomorrow because if you complain to Jack, imagine how Arthur is going to react. He's not known for being easy going and pleasant to work with," Lucy replied while going to put her mug in the kitchen sink."

The twins went off to bed, each consumed with their own thoughts. Lucy thinking about breaking up with Kaili and the possible repercussions. Belle obsessing about having to go to work the following day and what was going to explode.

And, as foreseen, a volcano did erupt.

chapter three

The Animal Awareness and Control Department was part of the larger council offices. It took up about a third of the first floor, sharing with two other departments. It was an open spaced area with horrid maroon barriers creating cubicles for each employee plus a separate soundproof room for the noisy photocopier. A lucky few had window views but there were the normal arguments about the sun shining on the computer screens so the blinds tended to always be down regardless of the season. Belle was one of the lucky few and her blind was raised about twenty centimetres so she could see outside if she leant down and twisted her head. Lucy sat at the reception desk which was really just a hole in the wall where people with questions could try and find some help.

There were ten people in the "Animals" Department as it was affectionately known. Mark Carter was the head of several departments including Animals while Jack Taylor led the actual Animals teams.

Short, round and bearded, Mark Carter was totally focussed on succeeding. This has left him in his forties, divorced and having little contact with his two daughters.

On the flip side, Jack Taylor was tall. Really tall when measured against the rest of the people in the office. Tanned and fit from swimming and running, many people overlooked his keen intelligence concentrating only on the handsome outer package. Jack was the youngest of three sons and, as a result of his upbringing, calm and relaxed with an easy sense of humour. This combination of quiet intelligence and good looks caused many unwitting broken hearts and was the perfect foil for Mark.

Lucy was the receptionist (and unofficial Personal Assistant for Mark) plus there were three people in the Awareness team and four people in the

Control team. Belle was one of the Event Coordinators in the Awareness team.

Belle and Lucy walked into the office the following morning, both yawning from the previous late night. Jane King accosted them the minute they walked in the door.

"What have you bought for morning tea?" she asked, noticing their empty hands, "Everyone was supposed to bring something. I bought Red Velvet cupcakes with Chantilly cream icing."

Jane King was a strange mixture of personalities. She had been with the council for a long time but had given up on expecting any promotion. She was also very old fashioned and self-centred. Short, dumpy with grey curly hair, she made some of the best scones from the CWA and with her husband long dead and daughter estranged, she brought in leftovers for office morning teas.

"Good Morning to you too," Belle replied sarcastically.

Everyone in the office had been the target of Jane's cruel tongue; obviously it was their turn. Jane had so many strong opinions and was quick to express them. She was also quick to start gossip; whether it was based in fact or fiction. She had previously accused Kevin Wallett of stealing council resources, Arthur Douglas was apparently cheating in his job and her latest stories intimated that the boss, Mark, was involved with insider trading.

Belle walked to her desk without answering Jane's question, while Lucy (still always the peacemaker) explained they'd bought dip and biscuits in yesterday and these were in the fridge ready for the morning tea.

"Morning all," Belle called out to the rest of the Awareness team, throwing her handbag in her bottom drawer.

Both other members of the Awareness team replied quietly to Belle's greeting; Arthur Douglas, an Event Coordinator like Belle, and Kelly Thompson, a part time Assistant who was there to help both Belle and Arthur. The Awareness team mainly focused on finding and implementing ways to make sure council residents were aware of their rights and responsibilities in relation to their animals.

Arthur Douglas was skinny, gaunt with grey thinning hair, a defeated expression and was quick to take credit for work he hadn't done. As an older person struggling against youth and time passing, he was often in conflict with his younger work colleagues. Very devoted to his wife and kids, he had overwhelmingly staid views which were tied to his religious beliefs.

Kelly Thompson was the opposite of their new team member, Paige Raynor. Only senior by ten years, she was decades older in experiences. Kelly Thompson was a single mum with two daughters, five and seven. Quiet, serious and tired with a washed out expression, she only worked to earn money to support her family but she was a very good colleague and well-liked by all.

"What time is the meeting this morning?" asked Arthur, not bothering to check his diary.

"9.00am," out of habit both Kelly and Belle responded.

Everyone followed their morning routines and proceeded to turn on computers, check any email that had arrived since yesterday and it was soon time for the meeting.

When Belle and Kelly walked into the conference room for the status meeting, Jack was already using his recent project management training to put together a plan on the whiteboard with headings for all the tasks that needed to be done and by when.

The conference room was attached to Mark's office and was used by both teams for meetings. Painted council grey, it had a rectangular table in the middle of the room which seated fourteen people comfortably although it rarely held more than ten. There was a computer connected to a large screen on the wall for presentations plus a smaller electronic whiteboard near the adjacent wall. Artwork was hung on the other two walls, changing on a regular basis with different prints from other council walls.

Grabbing a seat at the side of the conference table, Belle shuffled her papers in front of her so she could easily show what tasks had been done. Kelly sat beside Belle and gazed at the print on the opposite wall.

About ten minutes passed before Arthur entered the room and made a huge production about sitting at the head of the table. He looked at the whiteboard and rolled his eyes, all this training made so much extra work. There was nothing wrong with how they used to do it. When everyone was settled, Jack turned from the whiteboard and asked, "Where are we up to?"

Belle started to respond when Arthur spoke over her, "I've contacted the mayor and he's happy to open the expo."

Belle interrupted, "Thanks for doing that for me, Kelly has been in touch with three local vets and all have confirmed they will do the micro chipping.

I've also arranged advertising with the local paper and contacted the IT department to include the details on the council website."

"Belle asked me to prepare a flyer which will be mailed out to all the residents and that's ready to go. I just need to confirm the mailing list," said Kelly.

Jack made notes on the whiteboard, "What exhibitors have agreed to participate?"

Belle and Arthur started to speak at the same time. Jack said, "Arthur?" while Belle glared at them both.

Arthur listed the pet stores and businesses that he had contacted and who had agreed to take part; conveniently forgetting that Belle had identified all the different possibilities, found all the contact details and provided a script for him to follow during the phone calls.

Jack listed these exhibitors on the whiteboard, "This is good. What's left to be done?"

"I've got everything under control," replied Arthur with a smug little smirk on his face as if daring Belle to contradict him. She couldn't decide if he thought this was being funny or if he actually believed this was the way to behave. She looked at Kelly who just shrugged as if to say, 'Here we go again.'

"Good work Arthur," said Jack.

Belle sat there seething. She was so angry she didn't know where to start. The absolute laziness of the man or the flat out lying. Taking three deep breathes and trying to remind herself that she wanted to be professional, she looked down at her papers.

"So, Arthur what exactly needs to be done?" Belle queried, knowing full well that Arthur had no idea.

"Um ... well ... All the things we discussed last week."

Seemingly unaware of the rising tension in the room, Jack looked over from the whiteboard, "Good idea. Let's list all the outstanding tasks and work out when they need to be done by. Arthur, what's the next thing you're doing?"

Belle sat there silently gloating, hoping Arthur would finally fall on his face.

"Belle, have you got that list in your pile of papers?" Arthur asked with another smirk.

"No, I've only got the list I wrote."

"Well we can start with that ..."

"No, if you've got it under control, we should use your list."

Jack raised his head finally acknowledging the barely concealed friction, "Forget the old lists; let's make a new one now. What's the next thing we need to do?"

Belle glared at Arthur daring him to come up with a task. There was an awkward silence until Kelly quietly said that she needed to confirm the mailing list for the flyer. Jack noted that on the whiteboard. After a slow start, they finally ended up with the list of outstanding jobs and agreed who was doing which job and by when.

Jack printed four copies from the electronic whiteboard, "Let's meet again at the end of next week and see what progress we've made. But now it's time for morning tea and those red velvet cupcakes that Jane has been raving about."

Belle was very unhappy with the task allocation, especially the main job of creating a placement map. This was the task that pulled the whole expo together and Jack had given it to Arthur. What was going to happen when Arthur did his normal half-hearted job and everything fell in a hole? Jack had refused to listen to her opinion and so Arthur got the key job. She snatched her printed copy from Jack and left the room plotting revenge on Arthur. And maybe Jack at the same time.

chapter four

Morning teas were held each month in the office to celebrate birthdays occurring in the coming four weeks. Strangely in November no-one had a birthday but there was still a morning tea. While Jane was the instigator of these events (and loved to show off her baking expertise), everyone from the Animals department was invited. So in addition to the Awareness team, Mark, Jack, Lucy and the Control team were included.

The Control team spent most of its time collecting dog registrations and following up barking complaints. It was amazing how many people liked to complain! They also managed the dog parks within the council area and organised weekly dog training for residents. Due to the latest budget cuts there were only three Animal Control Officers for all this work plus Jane as an assistant.

Paige from Jules's class was the newest recruit while both Frank and Kevin had been around a long time.

Frank Morgan was a fifty three year old Australian Football League fanatic with short grey hair and ruddy skin from his obsession. He was disgruntled with work, having reached his peak and then stalled. Frank's wife had her own life and their adult kids have moved interstate. His favourite (and only) past time was AFL, refereeing kids' games, going to home games or watching his team on TV. He was looking forward to retirement and his dreams of more AFL involvement.

Kevin Wallett was a stereotypical computer nerd. At forty seven he still lived at home with his mum and dad and only worked to have enough money for the latest technical gadget. He was just under six foot tall with long grey streaked hair and his love of computer gaming explained his overweight size and pasty complexion. He and Frank had developed a strange friendship based on lack of motivation and sloppy work habits. And now after only a few months, their apathy seemed to be rubbing off on Paige.

Jane's contribution to the morning tea this month was those red velvet cupcakes and they disappeared as soon as everyone gathered. The rest of the contributions consisted of packets of store bought biscuits, a couple of dips and a sorry looking lump of cheddar cheese.

While everyone was nibbling at the remaining food, Jane clapped her hands together and announced, "It's time to sing Happy Birthday."

"But no-one has a birthday in November," replied Lucy.

The rest of the team ignored Jane and continued with their own conversations. These were the only occasions when the rest of the office considered it worthwhile putting up with Jane in exchange for her baked goods so once the cupcakes were devoured, any influence Jane had, vanished quickly.

After the normal social chat, talk naturally turned to the upcoming event. Specifically all the different dog colouring pictures they'd received from the neighbourhood kids.

"It was a really good idea to have a colouring competition to decide which dogs are the doggie taste testers. Everyone seems to want their dog to be in it and the entries are flooding in," said Lucy, "Well done Belle."

"It was a team decision," replied Arthur, "And we're very happy with the positive response."

Belle looked at Lucy and just shook her head with a rueful look on her face; this Arthur take down needed to happen soon. Maybe her friends would have some ideas.

"How many entries have come in?" asked Paige.

"Over two hundred so far and the competition doesn't close until Friday." As receptionist, Lucy was keeping a tally and storing all the entries until next week when Mark, Jack and Lucy would decide on the final twenty doggie taste testers.

"Have you got a favourite yet?" Paige teased Lucy.

"You know I'm not allowed to but there was a gorgeous picture of this black and white Border Collie that came in last week," laughed Lucy.

"Kelly are your kids entering Dexter?" asked Paige.

"They can't – that's cheating! Imagine if someone found out that one of us won the competition; how would that look," Jane exclaimed.

Kelly turned red and looked directly at Paige, "No the kids know they can't enter even though they did want Dexter to be a taster."

"As council employees we're not allowed to enter these competitions," Belle explained quietly to Paige who nodded silently and went back to her desk, pulling out her mobile phone.

"But I suppose it's not the first time Kelly's children have been in trouble for cheating ...." mused Jane, seemingly to herself.

"Shut up Jane," said Frank, "You don't know what you're talking about."

"Don't you tell me to be quiet. You're another one with a history of cheating. How would you like your wife to find out about Helen?" Jane threatened loudly.

Frank and Jane stood glaring at each other while Kelly looked as if she would die from embarrassment.

The loud voices roused both Jack and Mark from their intense discussion about the stock market. Mark decided this was a good time to leave while Jack stood and looked at Jane's flushed cheeks and wondered what she'd done this time. Jack had tried everything he could think of to improve Jane's work performance but she always thought she was right and that everyone else was wrong. She was just not suited to working in a team and it was wearing him down.

"Time to get back to work," Jack interrupted the staring contest, "Jane, could you please clean up and Frank, I need those complaint numbers by lunchtime. Kelly could you please start copying the guides for new pet owners, we'll need two hundred for the expo."

"The photocopier is playing up again," replied Lucy, "I've contacted the service department and they should be here today."

"Put a sign on the door to the room and then when it's working again, let everyone know."

Everyone dispersed to their own desks while Jane took the plates and cutlery to the kitchen to clean them. Putting the dishes away in the cubicle behind Paige's desk, Jane heard a voice coming from the other side of the barrier and stopped to listen. She opened the fridge door and leant towards the voice on the pretext of removing a drink.

"When can I get them?" Paige asked looking around for anyone listening, "I'm going out tonight and really need them."

There was a murmur from the phone and then Paige said, "I'll see you about 10.00pm then."

Paige returned her phone to her handbag, stood up to stretch and saw June standing with the fridge door open.

"What are you doing?"

"Just getting a drink."

Paige moved to blocked Jane in the spare cubicle and glared at her.

"What did you hear?"

"Nothing."

As Jane pushed past Paige, the cranberry juice she was carrying splashed on Paige's cream silk blouse.

Paige looked down at her blouse, pulling it away from her body, "No!"

"Don't get your knickers all in a knot. It will wash out."

"This is silk! It doesn't 'wash out'!"

"Well you shouldn't have blocked my path."

Jane quickly scarpered back to her cubicle and buried her head in papers on her desk to stop the conversation. Paige looked from her blouse to the top of Jane's head and back again.

If looks could kill, Jane would be six feet under.

chapter five

The next day did not start well for Lucy.

After a busy day at work, then staying up late to watch Belle's latest TV favourite, she forgot to set her alarm and of course, slept in. Normally this would not be a problem, she would just be a bit late but Lucy's car was with the mechanic so Belle was driving them both. Belle did not like to be late. She routinely left early just to make sure she was on time and was not tolerant of Lucy's more casual attitude.

So Lucy's morning began with Belle stomping around the house, looking at her watch regularly while Lucy rushed to get ready.

They finally got to work with a minute to spare and everyone else also seemed to be in a bad mood. The office environment was very sullen but thankfully quiet as people sat at their desks involved in their own problems.

At 9.00am exactly, Lucy opened the front counter and there was already a line forming. She spent the next thirty minutes directing people to the right place or providing the reams of forms that the council seemed to love. Finally she was serving the last person in the line; a tiny old lady, about five feet tall and no more than skin and bones.

"Could you please tell me what sort of dog I should buy?" she asked.

"I'm sorry, the council can't say what sort of dog you should have. Perhaps you should go to Animal Welfare; they might be able to help."

"But the council has always helped me before. She helped me pick out Freddie when he was born."

"Freddie?"

"Freddie was my last dog. He was a Chihuahua and the girl who was here before said to pick the one with the longest ears. Said they were the easiest to train and Freddie was perfect."

"How long ago was that?" asked Lucy, worried the lady was going to burst into tears.

"Freddie lived until he was sixteen years old so nearly sixteen years ago."

"I'd love to be able to help you but my boss wouldn't like it."

Kind-hearted Lucy felt awful as the old lady walked away with her shoulders slumped. Maybe she should have made a suggestion. The rest of the day's questions were just as tiring; people with problems who wanted Lucy to solve them – whether they had anything to do with her or not.

The final straw happened at the end of the day. Noah Bradley had just arrived with his handcart laden with boxes of envelopes to deliver an emergency stationery order. He normally only delivered on Mondays and Tuesdays but one of the other departments they shared offices with had missed the cut off time and arranged an extra delivery.

Noah was tall, muscular and very fit from all the physical work needed for his job at a stationery company. He had little ambition in his work but was a very enthusiastic competitor in all the different sports he played. He was very protective of those close to him, particularily his mum, who raised him and his younger sister after his dad died when Noah was five years old. He and Lucy had been mildly flirting for a while now.

Just as Lucy was signing for the delivery, Arthur walked to the desk. He was obviously starting to feel the strain of actually having to do some work and when the photocopier wasn't working again, he finally snapped.

"Do you ever do your job? Sitting here chatting up a customer while the rest of us suffer because of your incompetence. The photocopier is not working again and you've done nothing about it," he bellowed, "Well what do you have to say for yourself?"

Lucy and Noah stared at him, embarrassed for both him and themselves. Lucy stood and tried to calm Arthur down, "The service technician came yesterday afternoon and a new part is needed. They've ordered it and the copier should be fixed by the end of the week."

Arthur grunted.

"I've made an 'Out of Order' sign and put it on the door and everything should be fixed soon."

Arthur left without a word while Noah shook his head, "Why do you put up with that?"

But before Lucy could explain, Jane approached the front desk, "All this nastiness could have been avoided if you'd just done your job. You know Arthur has a short temper; everyone knows this; it's why he never got promoted and there was also that blow up a couple of years ago. He was lucky to get away from the police that time but regardless part of your job is to make sure this office runs smoothly for all of us."

Lucy just turned away.

Jane continued, "And you shouldn't be chatting up strangers during work time. You know you can't use work time for personal things even if others like Kevin do but I suppose if Mark uses his time to make money from stock market information, what can you expect. And you're supposed to have a boyfriend even though I've heard you're having trouble with another one. Why can't you keep a man?"

Noah's jaw dropped and he stood with his mouth agape – what can you say to such a horrible person who had at the very least insulted (if not slandered) three people in one outpouring. Lucy's face was the red of a ripe tomato; you could practically see the steam coming out of her ears.

"As long as Jack is happy with my work, it's really none of your business," Lucy replied through gritted teeth, "And as to the rest of your nonsense, I suggest you concentrate on your own problems and stop butting in where you are not wanted."

"How dare you?"

"You have the nerve to ask me that?" Lucy's voice was becoming so shrill that shortly only dogs would be able to hear her, "You are a nosy unhappy woman who's only satisfied when you're interfering!"

The volume had progressively increased and everyone in the office was listening to the argument with avid attention. Most people were silently encouraging Lucy but reluctant to get involved. Just as Jane was about to respond to Lucy's diatribe, Jack approached the front desk with trepidation, "Is there a problem here?"

Both Lucy and Jane muttered under their breaths. Jane returned to her desk, huffing all the way, while Lucy smiled sheepishly at Jack and Noah, "Sorry about that."

Noah quickly handed over his delivery, grabbed his handcart and left. Jack followed suit, hoping that was the end of it.

25

The day was eventually over but not without Lucy losing her normal easy going personality. Curled up on the couch with a big glass of her favourite white wine, Lucy dramatically said to Belle, "I'm going to kill someone."

"Anyone in particular? Or just a stranger off the street?"

"I can't decide between Jane and Arthur. They both deserve to be hanging from a tree, covered in honey with a bear eating them."

Belle laughed, "Where are you going to find a bear?"

"I'm sure the zoo will lend me one; it will cut down on their feeding bills."

"Good idea and he can always share Cooper's bowl."

But Lucy didn't laugh; she was too busy visualising tortured deaths for her horrid work colleagues.

chapter six

Friday thankfully passed quickly with none of the drama from the previous day and as always the weekend started in such different ways for the twins.

Belle approached weekends as a time to sleep in, slowly complete all those weekly tasks such as washing and cleaning and then relaxing in preparation for the week ahead. Whereas Lucy was up bright and early, getting the chores out of the way and bounding into whatever was her latest passion. Last thing Sunday night was set aside for relaxing.

As Belle lay comatose under her quilt, there was a quiet knock on her bedroom door, "Belle? Belle?"

"Ummph."

"Belle, I'm going out for lunch and I'll pick up the food shopping afterwards. Do you want anything?"

The twins kept a running food list on the fridge so whoever ended up doing the food shopping always knew what was needed.

"Nup."

Lucy crept out of the house, shutting the front door quietly. She'd swapped her car for many hundreds of dollars last night but at least she was mobile again. Kaili was meeting her at a local coffee shop in thirty minutes and she hoped the breakup would go as smoothly as possible. Lucy didn't really think that Kaili would be too upset but you never knew.

The coffee shop, with its tiled floors and metal table and chairs, was an upmarket meeting place for loads of different people; older wealthy people having a weekly outing with their friends, mothers catching up with other mothers while their kids from the local private school were playing their Saturday morning sports and even gym junkies getting a caffeine and sugar fix after their workouts. Kaili was waiting when Lucy walked in. He waved enthusiastically while she took a deep breath and moved toward him.

While Lucy was ending things with Kaili, Belle had finally dragged herself out of bed. Never one to get up before he had a reason, Cooper bounded out of his bed when he heard his food container being opened.

"Want to go for a walk after breakfast?" Belle asked him while having her first coffee of the day as the dog food disappeared.

After a long lazy walk, Belle and Cooper started on their weekend chores, at least Belle did. Cooper flaked out on the back lawn after his exercise and enjoyed the mild sunshine. By the time Lucy returned with all the food, the sun was close to setting.

"I'm exhausted," Lucy exclaimed as she put all the shopping bags on the counter.

"How about we put all this away and order a pizza then watch a movie?" Belle replied.

"Sounds good, it's been a horrible day,"

"Why?" What happened?"

While they put the shopping away, Lucy finally confessed to breaking up with Kaili. She told Belle all the details of the awkward lunch which ended typically with Kaili storming off and leaving Lucy with the bill.

"Say goodbye to the money you lent him," Belle said unsympathetically, "At least you can now flirt properly with Noah."

"How do you know about that?" Lucy whirled around from the fridge.

"Everybody at work knows. Did you think you were being subtle?"

"Ummm."

The pizza and the latest romantic comedy put Lucy in a better frame of mind and by the time the twins arrived at their parent's place for lunch the following day, Kaili was all but forgotten.

Sunday lunch for the twins was always at their folks. Sometimes their Dad cooked, sometimes their Mum - it depended on whether Laura Anderson was scheduled for a Sunday shift at the local hospital where she worked as a nurse in the Emergency Room. Sam Anderson worked as an electrician when he wasn't doting on his kids or playing golf. Both were looking forward to retirement and the opportunities that it would provide.

That Sunday Laura was busy in the kitchen baking an old fashioned roast chicken with all the accompanying vegetables. After saying hello to their Dad, the twins joined her in the kitchen carrying a bottle of wine; the only contribution they were allowed to bring. It was nice sometimes to be spoiled again.

"Hey Mum. Here's the wine."

"Thanks. Just put it in the fridge. Lunch is about half an hour away."

"Is there anything we can do to help?"

"Yeah, sit down and tell me about your week."

The twins looked at each other, mentally arguing about who was going to start. Belle lost and gave a recap of how the Pet Expo was progressing and Cooper's latest antics. Having known them since her girls were in school, Laura asked about their St Matthew's friends and Belle told her about Charlie's training regimen, Jules's latest mother-in-law problems and Georgie's animals.

Sitting down to lunch, the conversation moved to Laura and Sam's retirement plans.

"Less than five years then retirement here we come."

"It seems to be getting closer all the time, have you made any actual plans yet?" asked Belle.

"Only that we want to do some travelling. I suppose at the moment, we're just making sure we have enough money set aside so when it gets here, we can do what we want."

"Anyway, Lucy we didn't hear what happened with you this week?" asked Laura.

The twins looked at each other. Belle shrugged as if to say 'You'd might as well just get it over with'.

"Well I had a bit of trouble at work this week,"

"What trouble?" Sam went automatically into protective mode.

"Nothing major. Just a yelling match in the office."

Both parents looked relieved.

Lucy explained the arguments with both Jane and Arthur.

"It wasn't my fault," she whined, "They're horrible people. Jane sticks her nose into everything and always has to have the last word. Everybody is sick of her. And Arthur, well he's Belle's fault. If she hadn't picked a fight with him, he wouldn't have blamed me for the photocopier."

"Don't blame me for Arthur. He's the laziest person I've ever met and you agreed that I had to do something. You just don't like it because he yelled at you."

"Girls." Sam had refereed many such arguments in the years since the twins were born and he was unsympathetic, "Wherever you work, there's going to be people you don't like, so what are you going to do?"

"I actually have an idea," announced Lucy.

"What?"

"I want to do something that will improve the morale in the office. It used to be a great place to work. Everyone was happy but over the last year it's changed. You know what it's like, no-one wants to be there, everyone is grumpy most of the time and Mark is so caught up in himself, he hasn't even noticed anything wrong. I think Jack has seen it but he doesn't seem to know how to fix it so I'm going to give it a go."

"But what is your idea?" repeated Belle.

"I want it to be a surprise for you too. But it will be unusual and flabbergast everyone. I'm getting quite excited about this now. It's like breaking up with Kaili – once you know it's the right thing to do, it's only a case of working out the details."

"You broke up with Kaili?" asked Laura.

"Uh yeah, I forgot I hadn't told you yet," Lucy replied sheepishly.

"Good thing it's your turn to dry the dishes, you can tell me all about it. Come on." Laura started collecting the used dishes and headed towards the kitchen.

Belle and Sam glanced at each other and quickly removed themselves outside. As Belle listened to her father talk about his vegetable garden, she wondered if Lucy had calmed down from last week or if she still wanted violent ends for her work colleagues.

What was the surprise she had planned? And what did she mean by 'unusual'?

chapter seven

Monday bought a surprise, not for Belle and the rest of the office, but for Lucy herself. Just before noon, Noah visited her with an unexpected invitation to lunch.

"I was delivering next door and wondered if you'd like to get something to eat? We can just go to the canteen if you're busy?" he asked.

Lucy blushed and shyly nodded her head. Jane was walking past of course and just rolled her eyes. Lucy called out that she was going to lunch and left quickly before anyone could comment.

On Tuesday, lunchtime couldn't come soon enough for Lucy. She was madly hoping for a repeat of yesterday's impromptu meal. It had been nice to eat with someone who paid for their own lunch (and hers too) and was interested in more than himself.

One of Lucy's jobs was to collect the mail each morning but that day, other tasks meant she didn't get to it until 11.30am and even though she took longer than usual, she was back at her desk by noon, just in case. Unfortunately when Lucy returned she found that Mark had left several envelopes with directions for them to be delivered across the Council Offices immediately. With no sign of Noah, Lucy delivered the envelopes then decided to settle for a sandwich out in the sunshine.

Shortly after 2.00pm Arthur came looking for Lucy.

"I thought you said the photocopier was going to be fixed last week?" Arthur asked.

"It was. The technician came on Friday."

"Well why is the 'Out of Order' sign on the door again?"

"I don't know. Did you check? Jane was complaining this morning about the lack of paper. We're waiting on a paper delivery so maybe the machine is just out of paper rather than not working?"

Arthur and Lucy walked down the hall to the photocopier room. The 'Out of Order' sign was prominently displayed on the door. As they entered the room, they found the overhead lights turned off with the room eerily lit by the display screen from the photocopier.

Next to the photocopier was a pile of empty paper boxes with a foot artistically poking out.

Thinking there had been an accident, Arthur and Lucy hurriedly started to clear the boxes but they quickly stopped when the moved boxes revealed Jane's bloodied body and wide unseeing eyes.

Arthur lost all colour in his face and swayed as if he was going to faint or throw up. Lucy dragged him out from the room, closed the door and checked the sign was still in place. She grabbed a nearby chair and pushed him into it.

"You stay here while I ring the police. Don't let anyone in."

Lucy ran through the office ignoring the questions being asked of her.

She quickly dialled 000 and asked for the police.

"Someone's been killed here," she informed the operator.

"Do you need an ambulance?"

"No. There is some blood but her eyes … . You should see her eyes. We need the police." Lucy shuddered.

"I'll send someone immediately. What's the address?"

Lucy gave the operator the address as the others gathered around her desk. Jack and the Control team had witnessed Lucy's mad dash through the office and out of curiosity had followed her to the counter. They listened as she called the police and then clamoured for more information the second she put the phone down.

"What's happened?" asked Jack.

"Who's dead?" asked Kevin.

Paige and Frank stood nearby, eagerly waiting to hear.

"Jane's dead. I don't know how but there's blood on the photocopier room floor. The police will be here soon."

Stunned silence greeted this pronouncement. Lucy put her head in her hands and took some deep breaths. Late back from lunch with Kelly, Belle rushed up to the counter and put her arm around Lucy's shoulders.

"Luce, are you okay? Arthur keeps saying you found a dead body in the photocopier room. Kelly is with him now."

Lucy nodded, "I've rung the police but we'd better tell Mark before they get here."

"I'll do that," volunteered Jack and shortly returned with Mark in tow. There was a general sense of 'what do we do now?' pervading the office. Everyone was sitting around at the desks closest to the front counter as if moving away would break the bubble they were in.

Luckily sirens were soon heard in the distance, coming closer until they blared from the car park. The first two constables on scene quickly assessed the situation and called for backup. The office was promptly filled with people from a range of emergency services.

Every new arrival was scrutinised from behind a variety of documents as the council teams sat at their desks pretending to be okay with the situation.

The police were fast and efficient which reflected badly on society and the frequency of this situation.

The senior detective Sergeant Harris quickly took control of the situation, asking who was in charge. Mark reluctantly said he supposed he was.

They went to Mark's office while the rest of the staff kept an eye on what was happening. The police seem to be taking lots of photographs from the flashes appearing through the open doorway down the hall but no one was keen to venture closer to the photocopier room to see any further.

Eventually Sgt Harris and Mark emerged from his office. Mark came over towards them and said "The police need to interview all of you and I've said they can use my office. Once the police say it's okay, you can go home. I've spoken to the Mayor and depending on the police; the office will stay closed tomorrow and reopen on Thursday. Sergeant Harris will let me know their progress and what's happening and then I'll ring each of you tomorrow and tell you. I've answered their questions so I'm going home, who wants to go next?"

Sgt Harris (they never did find out his first name) had been standing there listening to Mark and taking in the reactions from the staff and interrupted "No, I'd like to talk to the people who found her first."

He was clearly the detective in charge with the looks of the stereotypical old school cop; early sixties, average height with close cut grey hair and a tidy beard.

Lucy and Arthur looked at each other and Lucy nodded her head to indicate that Arthur should go first.

As Arthur and Sgt Harris disappeared towards Mark's office, the rest of the group started towards their own desks to pack up so they could leave as soon as the interviews were over.

Typically Mark left immediately with no concern for the wellbeing of his staff while Jack seemed overwhelmed and unsure of what to do. It was left to Belle to make sure that everyone had a way of getting home and that someone would be there.

Arthur was still in with the police by the time everyone had packed up so they began to congregate at the closed front counter awaiting any sign that it was their turn for an interview.

The shock was passing and conversations between the team members slowly started. Everyone in the office was agog with the news that one of their own had been killed, right where they worked.

Everyone was gossiping trying to work out who could have done this. It eventually dawned on them that they were all suspects because it was unlikely that a stranger had managed to get into the photocopier room. This changed the tone of the chatter.

When Arthur returned to the office, he was bombarded with questions from his waiting colleagues.

"What did they ask you?"

"Did you find out what happened?"

"What took so long?"

The young police officer who had been sitting quietly nearby interrupted, "Next person please and Sir you can leave now."

Arthur nodded soberly while Lucy went to be interviewed.

Everyone tried to pretend they weren't consumed with curiosity. Frank and Kevin huddled in a corner discussing the coming weekend's sports offerings with one eye on the entryway. Kelly gazed into space while Paige was talking a mile a minute to anyone who would listen. Jack and Belle sat together and alternated between exchanging worried glances and listening to Paige's waffle.

Having packed his bag, Arthur grunted in the general direction of the crowd and left with little fanfare.

Lucy on the other hand returned from her interview with a flourish of noise and obvious anger, "Arthur dropped us all in it. He told the police that we all hated her and anyone of us could have killed her."

This was received with general groaning and people's anxiety levels rose palpably.

Lucy hadn't finished her dramatic pronouncements though, "But the police think I did it so no need for you all to worry."

The young police officer stood up looking to intervene but Lucy responded before he could speak, "I came with my sister ..." she said pointing to Belle.

"Okay but no discussing your interview."

"Who wants to go next?" asked Jack. Kevin and Frank both made moves towards the door with Frank eventually leaving the office.

"Kevin you can go next then Kelly, Paige, Belle and I'll go last and close up the office. Is that okay with everyone?" asked Jack.

Everyone murmured sounds of agreement while Lucy volunteered to start a pot of coffee. With coffee cups in hand the four women gathered around the small round table the teams used for morning teas and informal meetings.

The police officer was just in hearing range so Lucy didn't refer to her interview, instead they discussed different theories on how it happened. Lucy was asked again to recount how Jane was found.

"I feel bad now," Paige said tearfully, "I joked about her having a long lunch when she must have been lying there all the time.

"When did you last see her?" asked Belle.

"About 11.30am I suppose. She said she was going to the Ladies and I assumed she was sneaking off to lunch."

Kelly had been very quiet until now, "How did someone kill her in the photocopier room without any of us noticing?"

"No one goes into the room unless they are using the copier and the 'Out of Order' sign was on the door so after all the hassles we've had with the copier no one would bother going in. And that's another thing, who else but one of us knew about the sign?"

"It was lying on the table in the room so the murderer could have just seen it and decided to use it."

There was movement in the office as Frank and Kevin swapped places, with Frank quickly going home; taking advantage of the afternoon off.

The girls returned to their conversation with Belle summarising, "So Jane was killed between 11.30am and 2.00pm. Where was everyone during that time?"

"It was around lunchtime so no-one's going to be able to say where they were for the whole time," replied Lucy.

"Didn't you have lunch with Noah?" Paige asked Lucy, "I thought I saw his van in the parking lot."

"No, he didn't ask me today." replied Lucy, "I had a late lunch today by myself and before that I was out collecting the mail, delivering Mark's envelopes and then manning the front desk."

"What about you Kelly? Where were you?" asked Paige.

"I had a late lunch with Belle and except for that hour, I was in the office but I bet no-one could corroborate this," said Kelly.

"Same as me. And you?" Belle looked expectantly towards Paige.

"I was in the office all morning, had an early lunch at my desk then covered the front desk when Lucy went to lunch."

"All we've proven is that any of us could have done it during either our lunch breaks or while we were supposably in the office." Belle sounded very disgruntled.

Kevin approached the table and interrupted, "Kelly, your turn."

"That was quick."

"Yeah they just wanted to know where I was and if I knew anything. I didn't so it was really short. See you all when we can come back." And with that he collected his things and left. The young police officer just shook his head in defeat.

Kelly left for her interview as Paige said, "And then there were three."

"Don't forget Jack."

They looked towards the middle of the office where Jack was sitting at his desk gazing into space. The conversation stalled with each of them lost in their own thoughts. It wasn't long before Paige went to be interviewed then finally it was Belle's turn.

When Belle returned from her interview, she was showing all the signs of red hot anger. Lucy jumped up from her desk, "What happened?"

"Let's go home." Belle replied flatly, looking towards the police officer.

They said their goodbyes to Jack and as he went for his interview, the twins left the building. As they got in the car, Belle looked over to Lucy and said, "You were right. I've got no need to worry. The only thing I need to do is schedule prison visits in my diary. You're their suspect and it didn't sound like they're looking anywhere else."

Lucy dropped her head and said "Shit."

chapter eight

We need to investigate," Lucy announced dramatically.

The rest of the group looked up from their meals, each glancing at the others, not knowing how to respond. They had already spent much of the night discussing the murder.

It was their usual Tuesday night dinner. All five friends had gathered in a local Asian restaurant and the twins had provided the topic of conversation for the evening. Luckily the restaurant had polished wooden floorboards and cafeteria like tables and chairs so the noise level was such that it was difficult to hear each other let alone another table.

It was after the second course of a three course banquet had been served that Lucy made her wild pronouncement.

"The police are responsible for this, not you." said Charlie, always the loyal police officer.

"But they think I did it" replied Lucy.

"Just let them get into it and they'll see you didn't."

"I can't take that chance; you should have seen how that Sergeant Harris grilled me."

"Aren't you being a bit melodramatic? Sergeant Harris is a good guy, a bit old fashioned maybe but he gets results."

"Well I'm going to try myself cos I don't think I'm going to like his results this time."

"How can we help?" Georgie asked eagerly.

"You can't help," interjected Charlie, "Leave it to the police."

"It won't hurt if we just ask a few questions, said Belle.

"Yeah it's not like we're going to interfere with the police investigation, we'll just ask around," said Lucy, "Alright so what do we do first?"

Charlie rolled her eyes at them and concentrated on the plate of food in front of her, determined not to encourage this foolishness.

"We need to find out where everyone was at the time it happened," suggested Belle.

"When did it happen?" asked Jules.

"Well, she wasn't there when I went to get the mail and that was about 11.30am. We just thought she'd gone for an early lunch without telling anyone, which she often does," replied Lucy.

"When was she found?"

"Arthur and I found her just after 2.00pm so she was killed between 11.30am and 2.00pm. This gives us the window of time when the murder took place so we need to find out where everyone was then. And we already know where Kelly and Paige say they were."

"The next thing to look at is why someone would want to kill her," said Jules.

"More to the point who didn't want to," joked Belle.

"Are we assuming it was someone in the office?" asked Georgie.

Belle and Lucy exchanged a serious look. It wasn't nice to think that someone they know and worked with every day was capable of killing but what else could they think?

"You need to have a security tag to get into the office so unless we find a stranger was let in, I think we have to assume that someone in the office did it."

"Who are we going to include as suspects?" asked Georgie, really starting to get into this.

Belle considered this question, "If we just take the office staff we have Mark, Jack, Arthur, Kevin, Frank, Kelly, and Paige. That's assuming that neither Lucy nor I are suspects."

"Well I can vouch for me but I'm not sure about you," Lucy's joke fell flat and earned her glares from around the table.

Jules's organisation skills took over as she pulled her tablet from her briefcase. Food was forgotten as she pushed her plate aside and opened her tablet.

"Give me those names again and I'll start a spreadsheet."

Belle repeated the names of her colleagues while Jules typed them.

Lucy started biting her lower lip, "I really have trouble thinking of any of these people as a potential murderer."

"What if I add an unknown person to the spreadsheet? This way we won't miss anyone outside the office?" offered Jules.

So it was decided. Jules would manage a spreadsheet listing all the suspects and any information that was discovered about them.

Charlie, who had been silent to this point, asked, "No-one's said how she died."

This one question highlighted the seriousness of their mission. For everyone except Lucy, who'd seen the bloodied lifeless body, this dinner entertainment had been more practical than emotional.

Lucy repeated what she'd told the police, "I found Jane lying next to the photocopier with empty paper boxes toppled over her head. Next to her was lying a big stapler covered in blood. I'm guessing she was hit with the stapler and fell into the boxes."

"Are we doing the right thing by asking questions and looking around?" asked Georgie, doubt showing on her face.

"No." Charlie predictably replied.

"I don't see any other choice. If the police won't look past Lucy, we have to." Belle flashed a tight smile at her twin.

"I just want to know what happened," Lucy said.

"I'm in," Jules reaffirmed. "What's our next move?"

Charlie shook her head in frustration but kept her opinion to herself. The other four friends started a lively discussion and after much arguing, it was decided that the first things they needed to find out was where each person was during the critical time and if they had any reason for wanting Jane dead. Belle and Lucy agreed to subtly question their colleagues. Belle would tackle Arthur, Kelly, Frank and Kevin while Lucy would talk to Mark, Jack and Paige. Hopefully they could get the information without anyone discovering their mission.

"But what do we really know about the private lives of these people, only what they tell us and who knows if that is the truth," asked Lucy.

Georgie, who was feeling pretty much left out until this point, offered to search online and see what information about these people lurked within social media. Belle wasn't sure if her colleagues were the right generation for this but agreed that all avenues needed to be researched. Jules emailed the suspect's names to Georgie just as dessert was being served.

At this point, dessert overtook investigating. Fried ice cream with chocolate sauce was not to be interrupted by anything! After dessert everyone started making moves to go home. Belle, Lucy and Georgie promised to call Jules as soon as they discovered anything; interesting or otherwise.

They made their way to the car park and were saying their final goodbyes when Lucy quietly asked, "Are we on the right track Charlie?"

Charlie had spent most of the night alternating between shaking her head and ignoring the chatter and was reserved when saying good night.

"Luce I'm a police officer. I can't help you with this. It would cost me my job if my boss found out I was helping a bunch of vigilantes."

"We're not vigilantes, we're just going to find out some inside information and then you can give it to your boss and chase it up," Lucy protested.

"I'm not giving my boss anything and you're not giving me anything. I'm having nothing to do with this."

Belle interrupted before Lucy could continue her entreaties, "Charlie's right. She needs to stay clear but I'm sure if we find out something interesting, we could run it past her ..."

All four friends looked expectantly towards Charlie.

"Officially, no. Unofficially, maybe ..."

The rest of Charlie's reply was smothered by a big bear hug from Lucy.

On the drive home Lucy and Belle were both very quiet, caught up in their own thoughts. But their thoughts were the same, "What have we got ourselves into?"

chapter nine

It was a very subdued group that gathered in the office early on Thursday morning for Mark's pep talk. He'd rung everyone the previous day and asked them to be at the office at 8.30am. As he spoke about the lack of progress by the police, he looked uncomfortably at Lucy and said that Jane's family was taking her body back to Whyalla for burial.

He offered time off for anyone wishing to attend the funeral in Whyalla but after some general muttering and no volunteers, it was decided that a wreath would be sent on behalf of the office in place of anyone representing them in person. Bizarrely, Lucy was delegated to arrange the flowers and buy a card.

It was difficult to tell if anyone in particular was acting strangely because they all were. It could have been due to the death of a colleague, guilt because they did it or just guilt because they disliked Jane and work was going to be more pleasant now she was gone. No-one asked any questions or interrupted Mark which was very unusual.

At the end of the meeting everyone seemed lost as to what they should be doing and there was a lot of staring aimlessly at computers. Jack eventually jumped up and started to give everyone a gee up and find out where they were up to with preparing for the Pet Expo. With a shake of his head he reiterated what Mark said about the senior executives having decided that the show would go on so they had to get all the jobs done. He asked Belle to meet with everyone concerned with the project and check on the progress then dish out the left over jobs while he, Mark and Lucy decided on the competition winners.

Soon after this, Belle approached Arthur's desk with trepidation; both because this was her first murder suspect questioning and also because Arthur was difficult to deal with under normal circumstances.

"Hey Arthur, Jack asked me to check how everyone is going with their expo tasks. Where are we with the catering? Have the permits been arranged for all the food vans? Have you drafted a placement map for the park showing where everything will be?"

"I've done everything Jack asked me to do."

"So all the food stuff is sorted out?"

"No-one has asked me to do anything with the food requirements so the answer is I don't know. You need to ask whoever is responsible for it."

"But Arthur, you agreed at our last meeting to look after the food vans, we wrote it on the whiteboard."

"Did we? Are you sure?"

"Yes I'm sure," Belle replied through gritted teeth.

"Oh well, we have plenty of time. I'll get it done on time." Arthur was more interested in reading his emails than talking to Belle.

Belle pulled out her copy of the whiteboard tasks and shoved it under Arthur's nose. Finally with his attention focused on the expo, they agreed (again) on what tasks Arthur was to do and by when. Belle told him she would check his progress in a few days and while she was putting her papers into a pile, she asked, "Arthur what time did you have lunch yesterday?"

"Why do you want to know?" Arthur immediately looked up from his computer and glared at Belle. Guilt was plain to see on his face.

"Just wondering where everyone was during lunchtime when Jane was killed." Belle blurted out not having considered how she was going to reply when asked this question.

"None of your business," replied Arthur, "I've already told the police and you don't need to know."

And with that, Arthur stormed off, leaving Belle sitting at his desk dumfounded with no choice but to return to her own desk. Her first murder suspect interview was over before it really started and it wasn't very successful. Although Arthur clearly had something that he didn't want her to know. Maybe the next interview would go better.

Later that day, Belle sat with Kelly in the conference room, looking over the brochures Kelly had gathered for the information packets. There was a pamphlet covering the rules for dog registration, advertising brochures from the sponsors and a map showing the locations of the council dog parks.

"Kelly, these are fine. Could you please photocopy each of these; maybe 100 copies ready for the packets?"

"Sure, once some copy paper has been delivered. I think that was the last complaint I heard from Jane. It will be strange without her griping," Kelly's voice was quiet.

"But will it be strange 'good' or strange 'bad' I wonder," Belle ruefully replied and picked up the other two documents, "How long has it been since these were updated?"

Kelly took the 'Guide for new pet owners' and 'How to combat barking dogs' from Belle and looked for the copyright statements at the end of the documents, "Years. I'll ask Kevin or Frank to have a look at them before they're printed. How many copies do you think we'll need?"

"Last year we had nearly 400 people attend the expo and everyone's hoping more will turn up this time so let's have 200 packets available. Actually, we'd better increase the photocopies of those other brochures too. We can always re-use later if they're not needed on the day. But leave these two documents with me, I'll ask Kevin and Frank about updating them."

That would give her an excuse to talk to them about their alibis, Belle thought to herself.

Kelly made a notation in her diary while Belle gathered the papers together, "Hey what were you doing before we had lunch yesterday?"

"Why?" Kelly asked distractedly.

"Just wondering."

Kelly looked up and rolled her eyes, "You're trying to find out who killed Jane."

Belle stared sheepishly at the table.

"And you think I might have bashed her? And then calmly had lunch with you?"

Obviously subtlety wasn't going to work with Kelly so Belle decided to be upfront, "No. The police suspect Lucy and aren't looking at anyone else so I'm just going to ask around. And I have to ask everyone just to be fair. Where were you?"

"I don't know. Around the office, nowhere particular and no I didn't kill her. Although there's a lot of people out there who are not sorry she's gone."

"Who in particular?" Belle asked, "And why aren't they sorry?"

"You know what she was like. Always sticking her nose in where it wasn't wanted. And she always had an opinion about everything and love to tell everyone the 'right' way to do things."

"Yeah and she did like to gossip."

"I don't know how she found out about people but she did. And then she held it over you always threatening to tell everyone."

"Sounds like she did it to you. Why, what did she have on you?"

"Nothing major." Kelly quickly evaded Belle's question with a shake of her head, "Her latest quarry was Paige. She was telling me last week that Jane was always eavesdropping on her phone calls and making comments so she's probably relieved that Jane won't be around."

"Anyone else?"

"Nothing new that I've heard. Just the old gossip about Arthur cheating at work, Frank's affair and Mark's insider trading."

"Was she talking about those again?"

"Yeah, didn't you hear her needling Frank at the morning tea last week? Anyway, have we finished here, I need to go and pick up the kids?"

"Sure. See you tomorrow."

Belle sat quietly at the conference table and thought about what she'd found out that day. Overall it had been a bust. Arthur refused to say where he was and Kelly saw through her questions straight away. Both of them seemed to have something to hide but was it murder or something else. Arthur was a possibility; he was mean and difficult to work with but did that make him a murderer? Belle didn't want to think that Kelly could have been involved but she was definitely keeping something quiet.

Belle considered what she would report to Jules; she couldn't really rule either of them out. Neither had alibis for the murder time and both acted weirdly enough that there was probably a motive of some sort she didn't know about. More work was needed with these two to find out the details.

But one bright spot of the day had been hearing the possible motives for Arthur, Paige, Frank and Mark. Or was Kelly just trying to send her searching elsewhere? How many others had a motive? Did everyone have a motive?

Belle lowered her head into her hands and wondered how much worse could this get.

45

After the failed team meeting and while Belle was unsuccessfully trying to discover the whereabouts of her group of suspects, Lucy was handed a golden opportunity to fast track her sleuthing when Jack told her that they were going to decide the competition winners today. This would put her in the same room as Mark and Jack so now all she needed was to figure out a way to raise the subject of the murder without being too obvious.

Lucy gathered her stuff and went to Mark's office to find his desk covered with applications. Lucy stood there watching as Jack tried to sort the pieces of paper into different piles while Mark kept exclaiming over some of the coloured drawings.

There were entries for two competitions; the first to have the family dog as a doggie taste tester and the second to find the best home cooked dog treat. Over three hundred kids had submitted entries for the colouring competition for doggie taste testers but thankfully only about a hundred written histories for recipes had been received.

On the actual day, there would be four rounds with eight cooks trying out their recipe each time so from the hundred submissions, they needed to select thirty two recipes. Then they needed four dogs for each round plus a new group for the finals so that totalled twenty doggie taste testers.

"Let's move everything into the conference room, there'll be more space on the big table," suggested Jack, picking up a batch of applications and moving towards the adjoining door.

"Don't forget that it's booked this afternoon," said Lucy, gathering up another batch of applications.

"Don't tell me it's going to take more than a couple of hours to sort this out," asked Mark, "I've got a meeting at 2.00pm with the Mayor to let him know what the police said and what we're going to do about the vacant position."

Mark stomped from behind his desk to the head of the conference table with a sour look on his face. Jack returned to the office and collected the remaining applications while reassuring Mark that they should be finished by lunchtime.

"First let's divide these into one pile for the colouring competition and another for the recipe competition."

As the three of them sorted through the papers, Lucy asked Mark, "What are you going to tell the Mayor? What did the police say?"

Mark stopped sorting and leant back in his chair pondering the question.

He looked up and saw Lucy listening intently to every word he said. Having an interested audience was a new (and pleasant) experience so Mark forgot any notion of confidentiality and everything the police had told him came flooding out.

According to the police, Jane had been really unlucky. On most people the one blow that was inflicted would have knocked them out but other than a monstrous headache, there wouldn't have been many after effects. The autopsy revealed that Jane had a particularly thin skull and unfortunately the blow landed right where it could do the worst damage and so she died.

The time of death had been narrowed down to between 11.30am when she was last seen and 2.15pm when she was found. Again, the autopsy had concurred with these times but couldn't really be more precise than that.

Lucy smiled to herself, they had already worked that out.

The big office stapler that had been found next to the body had been confirmed as the murder weapon. The stapler was one of those heavy duty ones that would go through wads of paper. It was about 50 centimetres long and weighed over 500 grams so anyone would have been able to lift it and strike the killing blow. The forensics people had found some blood and other body bits on its side but there were no usable fingerprints and some of the blood had been smudged.

Jack interrupted Mark's narration, "The entries are all sorted now so which contest shall we judge first?"

"The colouring competition. There's more entries but at least we don't have to read anything," replied Mark, always choosing the easiest path.

"What criteria are we're using to pick the winners?"

"Let's just throw them all up in the air and whichever ones land first, they're the winners," Mark joked, sort of.

Lucy picked up an original entry form and read the terms and conditions on the back, "It's the top five entries in each age group; 5 to 6, 7 to 8, 9 to 10 and 11 to 12. It needs to be an original form and then we need to consider neatness and originality but except for that, according to the rules it's really up to us."

"Let's split the entries into age groups and then each of us can individually pick our favourite top five and try to agree?" asked Jack.

Lucy and Mark murmured their agreement and as Lucy started to sort a pile of entries she asked, "If the police found the stapler with blood on it, wouldn't the killer have blood on their clothes?"

Mark returned to his leaning back in the chair position and replied, "The police said there was very little blood at the scene and it was possible that the killer didn't get any on him."

"They said it was a man?"

"I can't remember. I guess I just assumed it was a man. They did say it was probably a spur of the moment decision rather than a planned attack. The killer likely just lost their temper, picked up the stapler, thumped her and left. No noise. No blood. No more Jane."

Jack and Lucy grimaced at the image this conjured and the room was quiet as they each chose their favourite colouring entries. Agreement was reached quickly and the winning entries were set aside with a couple of reserves in case anything changed with the winners.

"What was the criteria for the recipe entries?" asked Mark.

Lucy picked up an original entry form again to read the rules, "Entries have to be 100 words or less and talk about the history of the recipe. Oh and each family was only allowed to enter one of the competitions, so we'll need to check that too."

"Let's divide them up then and start reading. The first person to read one checks the word count and writes the total on the top of the page and any over 100 words are automatically excluded and don't need to be read by the other two. We need a total of thirty two recipes."

Jack obviously wanted to get this job done quickly and with as little fuss as possible.

"It's going to take forever to read all of these," complained Mark.

"They're only 100 hundred words each. It will be quick if we just do it."

Mark's attention span was very limited and after reading a few entries, he reverted back to the topic of murder.

"The police have spoken to Jane's family and they didn't know of any reason for her murder and because it happened at work, the police were very interested in any disagreements here. That leaves everyone as a suspect because we've all wanted to kill her at some point."

Lucy was torn between finding out any scrap of information or finishing this job and escaping Mark's gallows humour.

Mark failed to realise that his audience didn't appreciate his jokes or musings and prattled on without thinking, "Come to think of it, they were very interested in you Lucy."

"Me? Why?"

"Someone must have told the police about all the arguments you had with Jane, because second time around they asked me a lot of questions about your relationship with Jane and what sort of person you are."

"That's not fair. Everyone had problems with her. Anyone could have had a reason to kill her. Jack, you were her boss and she gave you so many headaches. And I saw how she blackmailed you Mark. Why did you let her get away with all the stuff she did? Where were you two when she was killed? Who says you didn't do it?"

Subtlety took a flying leap when Lucy all but accused either or both of them of the murder. Both men scrambled to provide alibis for the critical time.

"I was with Jack then I had lunch over at the Plaza."

"I was in the office. Heaps of people would have seen me. I even had lunch at my desk."

"Yeah well I was at the front desk after delivering your envelopes then I had lunch too so don't be so quick to point fingers at me."

"We know you're not a killer Luce," said Jack soothingly "The police just need to follow up all possible leads."

The recipe winners were quickly chosen with little further discussion. As they were packing up all the papers, Mark pondered. "Even if it isn't one of us three, based on what the police said, someone in the office is the killer."

chapter eleven

J ules had dinner with Belle and Lucy that night.

The cooking styles of the twins were dramatically different and in line with their characters. Belle measured everything and followed the recipe to the letter while Lucy threw ingredients in the pot depending on what was in the fridge. This often led to a mish mash of dishes, some wonderful, some dreadful. Tonight's offerings were Lucy's vegetarian stir fry followed by Belle's Quick Chocolate Mousse. After a successful dinner, the three friends sat down in the loungeroom with coffees and a packet of biscuits to sort out where they stood in the investigation.

"Did you find out anything?" Jules asked.

Belle naturally went first, "Arthur wouldn't tell me his movements, said he'd told the police and it was none of my business. But I don't know if he was just being difficult or actually had something to hide. Kelly said she was around the office until we had lunch at 1.00pm so if she did it, the murder happened before 1.00pm. But she rightly pointed out that it would have been hard to murder Jane then calmly have lunch with me as if nothing had happened. Unless she's a psychopath."

"So, you don't think it was Kelly?"

"Um, I guess not but she's definitely hiding something. And maybe she is a good actor – I don't know. I don't want it to be her because I like her but there's nothing definitive to rule her out."

Jules didn't know either Kelly nor Arthur and was more pragmatic, "So we can't eliminate either of them yet. Lucy, were you more successful?"

"Not really. Both Mark and Jack said they were in the office, then at lunch. I think everyone is going to have the same sort of alibi. The window for the time of death is quite long so there's lots of opportunities for someone to pop into the copy room without being noticed."

"Well maybe we should look at motives then and see who had a reason to kill her," Jules suggested.

"Isn't being a nosy old cow enough reason to get her killed?" Lucy joked, "Then everyone has a motive."

Belle wearily shook her head while Jules said, "Maybe you shouldn't say that near any police officers? Things are bad enough already."

"Alright spoilsports. We have plenty of motives, there's Frank's affair, Mark's insider trading, Kevin using council resources, Arthur's temper and Kelly's kid cheating at school. If she threatened to talk about any of these, the person may have got mad enough to bop her over her head."

Jules checked her spreadsheet and asked, "What about Jack and Paige? Any motives there?"

"Don't forget us, we have motives as well."

Belle glared at Lucy, obviously tired of her flippancy, "Jack was having serious problems with her work performance, lots of arguing. And she and Paige had a run in last week where Jane ruined Paige's silk shirt. Plus, Paige was always complaining about Jane listening to her personal phone calls."

"Those motives don't seem enough to kill someone though."

"No but maybe there's something else there that we don't know about. And we also need to consider who was physically able to do the deed. Have the police said anything about how she died? Lucy, did Mark say anything to you?"

"He said that it was accidental, that someone just picked up the big stapler and conked her on the head with it. The police didn't say if it was a man or woman but they did say that Jane was unlucky to die. Apparently, it hit her in a particular place and for most people the blow wouldn't have killed them, her skull was just really thin."

"What about all the blood?"

"According to Mark, there wasn't much blood and the killer probably didn't get any on them. They think it was a spur of the moment decision to just thump her and unfortunately she died."

"That doesn't help with narrowing our suspect pool. Anyone could have done it. Anyway, what's our next steps?"

"We need alibis for Frank, Paige and Kevin. And we need to have a snoop around Jane's desk to look for anything unusual." Belle listed off the remaining suspects.

"Would she keep anything incriminating at her desk? Wouldn't she hide it at home?"

"Maybe, but it will be easier to search her desk first. Lucy, do you want to snoop? And do you think you can suss out Paige while I tackle Frank and Kevin? Then over the weekend we can tally up and see where we are."

"Sure," Lucy replied with little enthusiasm.

"I've had enough detective work for one night, I'm going to bed," Lucy announced as she picked up her coffee cup and headed to the kitchen, "Sleep well both of you."

Belle and Jules said goodnight as Lucy left the room and then Jules asked. "Is she doing okay? She doesn't seem to be taking it very seriously?"

"That's just her way of coping, I think she's more scared than she's willing to admit."

Once Jules had left, Belle picked up the dirty dishes, put them in the sink and let Cooper outside before going to bed. Maybe Lucy had the right idea, make a joke of it until the situation became dire. Surely the police wouldn't arrest an innocent person on circumstantial evidence? Maybe there was someone in her personal life who wanted Jane dead? Jane liked to ferret out secrets and maybe that ferreting got her killed. The TV crime shows always seem to get the right person in the end.

With all these thoughts floating in her mind, it took a while for Belle to drop off to sleep.

****

Friday dawned much too quickly and too brightly for the twins. The weekend was only one day away but felt like forever. As they dragged themselves to work, knowing what had to be done, the bright sunshine seemed to mock them, how could they continue to investigate the horrid events of this week on such a beautiful day. But how could they not?

The office environment was still subdued with little chatter but also little work being accomplished. A lot of staring at blank screens could be seen, with downcast faces just waiting for the weekend.

The Pet Expo still needed progressing though and Jack could be seen searching Jane's desk in a flurry, stuff going everywhere. "Has anyone seen the permits for the food vans? Arthur said he told Jane to organise them. And she said she'd done it. Where are they? We won't have time to reapply."

Lucy placed a calming hand on Jack's arm, "Let me have a look, they should be here somewhere."

She glanced at Belle; one stone, two birds.

As Lucy started to sort through Jane's desk, Paige offered to help. She opened the filing cabinet drawers and started to pull out each folder randomly and then returned it to its original place.

Seeing this, Lucy suggested, "Could you sort through her desk making piles for things that might be needed, things that can be reused like stationery, anything we need to return to her daughter like personal stuff and what can be thrown away while I look through the files to see if I can find the permits."

As Lucy tackled the filing cabinet, Paige sorted Jane's things into different piles. They worked silently for several minutes while Lucy covertly assessed Paige's demeanour. Paige was very pale with massive bags under her eyes, showing a clear lack of sleep and probable tears. Lucy's kind nature took over, "Are you okay?"

"I'm fine," Paige mumbled.

"I didn't realise you were so close with Jane. Where were you at lunchtime on Tuesday? Did you see something?"

Paige looked up from her sorting, glaring at Lucy, "Why are you asking me that? Why should I have seen anything? I suppose you think I killed her?"

The pitch and volume of Paige's voice rose with each question. Everyone in the office was now staring at them both. Lucy grabbed Paige by the arm and dragged her through the office and outside into the hallway.

"What's going on?" Lucy asked, "Why are you so upset?"

"Everyone is forgetting how horrible she was. No-one is remembering the nasty things she did to everyone. The police think she was a saint and no-one is telling them the truth."

"Well ..." Lucy started to reply but Paige continued ranting and pacing without hearing.

"I hated her. She was a miserable old bat who interfered where she wasn't wanted. You know, remember how she embarrassed you in front of Noah. She was always making nasty comments about everyone, about all the cheating; Kelly's kid, Frank on his wife, Kevin on the council, Mark on the stock exchange. She made coming to work horrible for everyone and I'm not sorry she's dead."

"But I didn't kill her," and with that, Paige ran out of steam and finally stood still.

Lucy stood beside Paige, "What nasty comments did Jane say to you?"

"She didn't approve of my lifestyle, thought I was mixing with the wrong sort of people and was always nagging me about being more responsible. What do I say to the police if they ask? If I tell them I hated her, I'm scared they'll think that I did it and I'll become their main suspect."

"The police think I did it, so I'm not sure you need to worry about that," Lucy replied, "What did you tell the police when they asked where you were?"

"Same as everyone else, at lunch or around the office."

Paige did not meet Lucy's eyes with this mumbled excuse but Lucy didn't see a way to refute it.

"Just tell the truth if the police ask, they must have found out what sort of person she was by now," Lucy advised, "Let's go and finish cleaning Jane's desk and then we can grab a coffee."

Lucy wondered what Paige was hiding. This detective lark wasn't as easy as it appeared in books. People didn't just tell you what you wanted to know.

chapter twelve

As Lucy and Paige were clearing Jane's desk, Belle was plotting her approach with Frank and Kevin. Neither man was particularly smart but both had the uncomfortable skill of seeing the exact point of any conversation.

Belle had told Kelly that she would arrange for Kevin and Frank to update the 'Guide for new pet owners' and 'How to combat barking dogs' so she had the perfect conversation starter. But where to go from there?

They needed to know where both Frank and Kevin were during the critical lunchtime period and also if they had any reason for wanting Jane dead, apart from the standard, 'she was a horrible person' reason.

Belle flicked through the pages of the 'Guide for new pet owners' as she pondered tackling them together or individually.

The 'Guide for new pet owners' was just that, although it did tend to focus on new dog owners. A lot of the information was still current because new pets still needed food, water and somewhere to sleep. The difference now was in the range of choices available to new pet owners. This reminded Belle that she'd better ensure that all sorts of different suppliers had been invited to the expo. She added that to her ever growing 'to do' list.

If she spoke to Frank and Kevin individually, they might contradict each other. Or more likely, wonder why she was separating them. No, better to speak to them together and just throw her questions in during the conversation and hope they didn't notice. But she'd better think up a reason for asking in case they challenged her.

The 'How to combat barking dogs' brochure would need more updating than the 'Guide for new pet owners'. The standard tips like exercising your dog, leaving a radio on for company and general obedience training were still relevant but there were many other options these days for keeping pups occupied and not barking such as treat toys, calming oils for anxiety and even machines where you could talk to your dog during the day.

Belle walked to their cubicles carrying the old brochures and interrupted their discussion about which cricket teams were playing in the coming week and what sort of chance they had. Although football was the major passion for most of the year, any sport would do when the footy season had just finished and the new season was still a few months away.

The impact of Jane's death seemed to be lessening here; was it because they had less to do with her or were they really that self-involved? Belle could see that Kevin who lived at home like a spoilt child might feel this way but she would have thought that Frank would have more empathy. It had only been two days but there seemed to be a level of acceptance from these guys that wasn't evident in other parts of the office or was it a front for one of them having killed her.

"Hey guys, would you be able to update these guides before they're printed for the expo?"

Frank was closest and took the two guides from Belle, "Why do they need to be updated?" He looked at the latest revision date and said, "It hasn't been that long."

Kevin had joined them and flicked through the Barking guide, "This seems okay. It'll be a lot of work to update them and who reads them anyway?"

"Guys, they're going to be updated. Both guides need to be looked at, checked to see if the information is still current and what else needs to be added. I thought you could take one each and have the final drafts back to me by next Wednesday?"

"Wednesday? That only gives us a couple of days?" complained Kevin, with Frank nodding his head in agreement.

"It's three days and that's plenty of time to update a brochure. Jane kept a list of queries received from the public so that might help you in deciding what extra information to include."

"But who knows where Jane's list is?" Kevin continued to complain, "The old bat was not organised."

"Old bat?" Belle queried, "What did she do to you?"

Kevin blushed, "Sorry, that was just habit."

"But there must have been a reason?" Belle pushed.

Kevin continued to flick through the Barking guide hoping that Belle would just change the subject but she continued to stare at Kevin until Frank lost his patience, "Jane was constantly hinting about everyone's secrets and last week was going on about how Kevin is always going to the stationery cabinet and stocking up. Kevin snapped at her and they were niggling at each other since."

"Until when?"

Frank suddenly looked uneasy, "Until she was gone."

Belle couldn't believe her luck. This was the opening she was looking for. She turned back to Kevin and asked, "So where were you on Tuesday between 11.30am and 2.00pm?"

Kevin sat miserably with his head bowed, "I don't know."

"Kevin was at his desk the whole time," said Frank, "I had an early lunch, left just after 11.30am and got back a few minutes before 1.00pm. Kev covered for me then ate his lunch at his desk when I got back, I saw him."

"But you really don't know where he was between 11.30am and 1.00pm because you weren't here. He could have been off killing Jane for all you know."

"I didn't kill her," Kevin weakly objected.

But Belle was on a roll, "Kevin had a motive and opportunity – that's the same as Lucy and the police think she did it."

"All of us had a motive," Frank spat, "She was a vindictive old cow."

"What was your secret then?" Belle threw caution to the wind.

Frank snorted derisively, "My secret is very old and very grubby. And while I would have preferred she kept her mouth shut, I certainly wouldn't have killed her to make sure she did."

"So where did you go on Tuesday if you weren't here? Can anyone vouch for you?"

"That is none of your business. If I need a witness, I'm sure that Paige saw me leave. She was in the carpark when I left, talking to some bloke through his car window. But that's police business, not yours. If you've finished nosing around, can we get back to these guides?"

Belle ignored Frank's sarcasm, "One more question: did either of you notice when the 'Out of Order' sign went up on the photocopier room door?"

Both Frank and Kevin shook their heads.

"Can you please send me the updated guides by Wednesday at the latest?" Belle started to leave then turned around, "Oh and I hear some people like snakes and rats as pets, please include a section in the New Pet Owner's guide for them?"

Belle sort of congratulated herself as she went back to her desk. Asking for the guides to be updated was going to be a waste of time. Any updating by Frank and Kevin would be superficial at best. Luckily she had enough time to proofread and redo the drafts herself if necessary.

But with the nosing around as Frank called it, she'd found out they both had a motive and the opportunity to kill Jane. Surely the police were looking wider than Lucy.

When she got to her desk, Belle found Lucy waiting, despondently scrolling on her phone.

"No luck?" asked Belle.

Lucy shook her head.

"Well in one way, that's good news. It means we can try and search her home. Did you sort out her personal stuff? We could return it to her daughter at the same time. Do you know if Mark has contacted the daughter? Do you know her name?"

"Her name is Jennifer King; I've got her phone number from the Next of Kin list we keep on file and I think she lives in the country somewhere." Lucy's voice sounded hopeless, "Mark mentioned that the police had notified her and she was coming to Adelaide next week."

Belle put her arm around Lucy and whispered, "Don't give up. We'll find something."

Lucy smiled wryly and leant back into Belle's hug.

Paige approached the twins, "Lucy, Noah is on the front desk phone asking for you."

"You go and see what Noah wants. If you leave Jennifer's phone number, I'll ring and see if she'll meet us."

As Lucy and Paige went to the front counter, Belle looked after them wondering how this Lucy and Noah situation would play out; happiness or sadness; or more probably a mixture of both. These thoughts led to her planned phone call with Jennifer King; was she going to be dealing with tears or temper; or maybe again a mixture of both?

chapter thirteen

Hello, is that Jennifer King?"

"Yes. Well at least I was before I got married. I'm Jennifer Petras these days."

"Hi I'm Belle Anderson. I used to work with your mother," Belle hesitated, "I'm sorry for your loss."

"Thanks, but it's fine. How can I help you?" Jennifer was quite matter of fact and to the point.

"Your mother was holding some papers for our upcoming pet expo and we can't find them. We know she was in the habit of taking things home sometimes and we were wondering if you could look for them at her place?"

Belle figuratively crossed her fingers. Hopefully Jennifer would let them search themselves but bluntly asking this would look rather suspicious.

"How urgently do you need these papers? I can't get to the city until next week some time."

"Unfortunately, we really need to look as soon as possible because if we can't find them, we'll need to reapply for the permits and time is running out to get the approvals."

"If you'd like to go and look earlier than next week, I could ring her landlord and arrange for a spare key. Would that help?"

"Thank you, that would be very helpful," Belle momentarily forgot they wanted to search for murder clues and started to problem solve, "If you ring him today, I could pick up the key on my way home, we could have a look over the weekend and reapply for the permits on Monday if we can't find them."

"Fine, whatever" Jennifer seemed to lose interest in the whole exercise.

"Also, we've packed up her personal things from work; would you like us to leave them in the house?"

"Sure, whatever."

"Is there anything else I can help you with?"

"Belle is it? I'm sure you're a very nice person, but my mother wasn't. I haven't seen or spoken to her in over two years. My husband is Greek and for that reason my mother objected to the wedding. Actually spoke up on the day when the celebrant asked if anyone objected and that was the last day I saw her. Our son has never met his grandmother and I haven't even spoken to her after she called him 'a little Greek boy' when I rang to tell her what I thought was happy news about his birth. If she's going to be missed, it won't be by me."

"Um …"

"The police say she was hit over the head with a stapler; I'm sure they have a long list of people who would have like to thump her, myself included. Luckily I was here in Whyalla hundreds of kilometres from Adelaide when she was hit but I really understand the desire to shut that mouth when it gets going."

"Err …"

"I understand I'm both the executor and a beneficiary of her will, so I should have no trouble getting her landlord to let you in. I'll ring today, the police gave me his details, and I'll tell him to expect you this afternoon. As to where anything is or even what is in her place, I have no idea but look as much as you want to and take what you need. My plan is to handle this as quickly as possible, sell everything, pay for the burial up here that my uncle is insisting on and donate the rest to charity. I don't need or want her money."

As Belle put the phone down after a short and uncomfortable goodbye, Lucy bounded up to the desk with a wide grin plastered across her face, "Noah asked me out for dinner tonight!"

Belle smiled wryly, "But you're coming to Jane's with me?"

Lucy's face dropped, "Is that tonight? Bugger. I suppose I can put Noah off."

"You can't reschedule, he might think you don't want to go," Belle laughed, "Anyway I wasn't planning to go tonight. All I want to do is order take away and curl up on the couch for the night. I'll pick up the key after work and we can go tomorrow."

60

"Great!" Lucy started grinning again, "I'm going to the Plaza at lunchtime and see if I can find something new to wear."

"Aren't you even going to ask what Jane's daughter said?"

"Uh … yeah … sure."

Belle quickly summarised the phone conversation.

"That certainly clears up why they were estranged," was Lucy's only comment, "Anyway, cover for me while I take an early lunch. It would be nice to find something to wear that blows Noah's socks off."

"Sure, I have to check on everything for the expo anyway and hopefully searching Jane's place tomorrow will tell us our next step there. Nothing exciting should happen if you disappear for an hour or so."

Lucy grabbed her handbag, waved goodbye and was out the door before Belle could change her mind. Belle moved to the front counter to relieve Paige. She carried her expo folder and silently wished for no customers so she could go through the checklist and sort out what jobs were being done and what else needed to either be done or handed out to someone else to do.

Shortly after 1.00pm, Belle momentarily left the front counter and popped into the kitchen to get her lunch from the fridge. As she returned to her temporary post, she noticed the police entering Mark's office. The door was shut with a resounding thud.

When Lucy returned at 2.00pm with several bags from her shopping lunch, Mark's door was still firmly shut. Belle filled Lucy in about the police visit and they were both staring towards the office when the door finally opened.

"Thank you for your help. We'll get set up in the Conference Room down the hall and if you could please send in the people as discussed that will be appreciated."

Mark nodded his head and they separated; Sergeant Harris and his colleague towards the Conference Room and Mark towards the general office. Belle and Lucy quickly looked down at some papers on the desk to hide their obvious interest in what was happening.

As Mark entered the general office, he cleared his throat to get everyone's attention, "The police have found some discrepancies, have spoken to me and want to clear up a few things. They want to speak with Paige, Frank and Arthur again. Frank, they're waiting for you in the

Conference Room. Paige, Arthur; I'm sure they'll tell Frank who they want to speak to next."

And with that Mark turned around and retreated to his own office. Frank stared after him and shook his head, "Our fearless leader; so kind; so supportive."

"Might as well get this done," Frank looked back at his colleagues, "Don't look so worried, I didn't kill her so whatever they want to clear up is going to be fine."

As Frank started towards the Conference Room he looked back, "Paige, Arthur; what about you guys? Anything to hide?"

Paige began to shake, Lucy walked over, put an arm around her shoulders and whispered, "Just tell the truth."

Arthur turned a bright shade of crimson, "What I do in my lunch hour is my business and no-one else's."

Belle watched Arthur with interest, maybe his alibi would finally be revealed.

"I was either in the office where everyone could see me or not on the premises during the relevant timeframe. I told the police this already."

"Maybe they just need more details about where you went when you left the office?" Belle both tried to confirm that he had indeed left at some point and stir the pot at the same time.

"It's none of their business where I went or who I saw," screeched Arthur.

Jack tried to reason with him, "I think you might find that the police consider everything is their business in a murder investigation. Would it be that bad to tell them where you went?"

Arthur dropped into a nearby chair, a picture of misery, "How do I explain? How do I tell them that I don't want my Mary becoming one of them?"

Jack sat down next to Arthur and waved his arm for everyone else to return to their work. Everyone went back to their desks but the silence was deafening, all ears were tuned in to this conversation.

Arthur, on the other hand, appeared to have forgotten the captivated audience and with a little prodding from Jack, the whole sorry story came tumbling out.

Arthur's daughter, Mary, turned 18 last month and had declared her desire to become a police officer. Arthur and his wife, Margaret, were appalled by the idea of their little girl dealing with the scum of society and were doing everything they could think of to change her mind. On the other side, Mary was standing firm and planning to join the force in the next intake.

Arthur had taken advantage of a quiet day and gone to his local church to meet with the Parish Priest to get some counsel and possibly some new ideas for tackling what he and his wife saw as a major problem in their family.

When Arthur returned from the church and the body was found, naturally the police were called. Arthur found himself in a dilemma because how could he explain to the police that his alibi was meeting with a priest to stop his daughter from joining the police. So, he just said that he'd been out for lunch at the Plaza but someone must have seen something and now the police were questioning his story. It was going to look so bad; firstly, that he hadn't been honest to start with and then what he was actually doing.

As Arthur ran out of steam, Frank returned to the office, "Arthur, you're next."

chapter fourteen

After Arthur's meltdown, Jack called off the pet expo status meeting and said he'd reschedule it next week. The rest of the day passed with no more excitement and eventually it was the much anticipated weekend.

Later that evening, Belle was sitting on the couch perusing a Chinese takeout menu when Lucy walked into the loungeroom in her new red jacket, "Do you think this is dressy enough?"

"Did Noah say where he was taking you?"

"To that trendy pub in the city for dinner then a movie," replied Lucy, checking her makeup in the mirror.

"You look great. Is he picking you up or are you meeting there?"

"He's picking me up," Lucy looked at her watch, "Any time now."

And as she replaced the compact in her handbag, the doorbell rang, right on time. Cooper started barking and jumped up from his bed just as Belle grabbed his collar, "Have a good time."

Lucy grinned "Don't wait up."

Lucy opened the front door, greeted Noah and they were gone in a flash. Belle smiled and looked towards Cooper, "Should we get Beef with Black Bean Sauce or Chicken Satay for dinner?"

After devouring her delivered Chinese dinner, Belle started to tally up what they knew about Jane's murder, what they didn't, what needed to be found out but very soon it was information overload. She needed to logically categorise all the information to find any gaps. She really needed to talk to Jules and add everything to the spreadsheet.

"Jules, can you talk for a bit?" Belle had rung hoping that Jules could spare a few minutes to help save her sanity.

"Sure, Drew is just leaving to have drinks with some of his footy mates," Jules lowered her voice, "I really think they miss getting together once the footy season has ended but they won't admit it."

"Could you get the spreadsheet up because I have a few things to add to it. Today has been rather interesting," Belle deadpanned.

Jules said goodbye to Drew, opened up the spreadsheet on her tablet and put Belle on speakerphone, "All right, fill me in."

"Lucy spoke to Paige and I spoke with Frank and Kevin. Plus, the police turned up again and wanted to re-interview Frank, Arthur and Paige."

"Did you find out any motives or alibis?"

"Both Paige and Kevin got really upset when we started asking. Paige went on a rant and Lucy had to take her out of the office. There was obviously lots of tension between them but Paige insisted that she hadn't killed Jane, that she hadn't left the office. And there wasn't a specific motive, more just hatred of each other and their lifestyles."

"And why did Kevin get upset?"

Belle hesitated, "He did get upset initially, calling her names and Frank admitted that they irritated each other all the time, right up until she died."

"And ... ?"

"I was the one who started ranting," Belle admitted, "Frank and Kevin were covering for each other and I got annoyed. All the evidence the police have which incriminates Lucy is that they didn't get on so when the guys bagged Jane then Frank said that Kevin couldn't have killed Jane, I lost it and said that there was the same evidence on Kevin as there was on Lucy."

"Oh Belle," Jules commiserated, "How did they respond to your rant?"

"Frank said that we all had a motive and he was right. If she was killed for being a horrible person, all of us had a reason for wanting her gone. But Frank did inadvertently confirm that he left the place for nearly two hours and if Paige did see him in the carpark, then he does have an alibi for a big chunk of the relevant time. But he wouldn't say where he'd been or if he had a particular motive."

"Okay I'll note that on the spreadsheet. Anything else?"

"I did ask Frank and Kevin if they noticed when the 'Out of Order' sign went up. They didn't notice but it might be important. If the murderer put it up after being in the photocopier room, it will reduce the timeframe."

"That's a good question. We should find out if anyone admits to putting the sign up or at the least, saw when it went up. I'll include it on the spreadsheet too."

"And something else to add, I spoke with her daughter, Jennifer, and she needs to be entered as that extra person. I don't really think she killed Jane but as she inherits and hated her mother, she does have the best motive and could be involved somehow."

"You've had a busy day," Jules commented as she typed the information onto her tablet, "No wonder your head is spinning."

"I haven't finished yet. We finally found out what Arthur's alibi is."

Belle relayed Arthur's sorry tale about his daughter and going to the church for help, "What sort of person is so selfish to try and stop their kid becoming a police officer?"

Assuming the question was rhetorical, Jules asked, "Is that it for today?"

"One more thing but I'm not sure how it can be added to the spreadsheet, or even if it should be added," Belle pondered, "The police turned up at the office today to reinterview some people."

"Who was reinterviewed?"

"Mark, Paige, Frank and Arthur. And after the interviews, they were all very quiet. There was no chatting about what was asked even when Jack tried to find out what was said. I think the police might have told them not to talk about it."

"I wonder why those four were chosen to be reinterviewed? They must have something in common," mused Jules, absently scrolling through the spreadsheet.

"I'm not sure," Belle replied, "Hold on while I grab another drink."

Jules continued to look at the information collected so far.

"I'm back," Belle announced as she picked up the phone again.

"Hold on," Jules said, "I think I see why the police reinterviewed Mark, Paige, Frank and Arthur."

"Why?"

"They were the only four to leave the actual building for lunch. Mark went over to the Plaza, Arthur went to the church, Frank wouldn't say where he went but he did say that he went somewhere and Paige was seen in the carpark so she must have gone somewhere too."

"But Paige said she hadn't left the office?"

"She must have lied. You said that Frank definitely saw her in the carpark talking to someone through a car window."

Belle flicked through the pages of notes written by both her and Lucy to see what they'd written about Paige. Both times she'd been asked where she was between 11.30am and 2.00pm, Paige had said she'd been in the office. And Frank's response had her in a different place for at least part of the time, so where did Paige go? Was it somewhere totally innocent or was she hiding a more sinister objective? Or was Frank lying? Maybe he thought that saying he'd seen Paige in the carpark would help his story? Which it actually did.

"You or Lucy will need to check with Paige and Frank again to see who's telling the truth," said Jules, "Who do you think is lying?"

"Umm I'd guess that it's Paige that's lying," Belle replied, "She did get so upset that they had to leave the office. But more interesting is what does leaving the building have to do with the murder? I wonder why the police are concentrating on Mark, Arthur, Frank and Paige?"

"No idea but that's the thing that jumped out at me from all the information so far," Jules continued, "Do we need to make any changes to our suspect list? Add anyone new or take anyone off?"

Belle considered these questions for a moment, "We've added Jennifer, her daughter, and we still have 'Unknown' sitting there if needed so I don't think we need to add anyone else. About taking someone off, I really don't think we've gathered enough specific evidence to say So and So didn't do it. Even though there's a couple of people I don't think could have done it, I don't know for absolute certain."

"What do you have planned next?"

"Lucy and I are going to search Jane's place tomorrow. We've told everyone it's to find the permits for the Pet Expo, and I do hope we find them, but I'm also hoping we might find something that gives us a new lead because we're sort of running out of places to look."

"And once you talk to Paige, it might be all over anyway, that is if she did it and confesses," Jules said, "I'll finish tidying up the spreadsheet and then I'll email it to you and you can see if anything pops out."

"Georgie and Oliver are coming over for dinner tomorrow night too so maybe Georgie has found out something from their online presence, although I'm not too hopeful with my technology challenged colleagues," quipped Belle, "Thanks for listening tonight. I'll see you for dinner on Tuesday unless the world blows up in the meantime."

"Night. Sleep well."

As Belle hung up the phone, Cooper stirred so she got up and let him outside to do his business before bedtime. She was making herself a cup of tea when her phone dinged, signalling the arrival of a new email. Belle opened the spreadsheet and started to look at the names of her colleagues, or suspects as she now called them. She skimmed over all the different motives and alibis they had determined and still nothing became clearer.

What had begun as primarily a bit of fun, was now serious with consequences too awful to contemplate.

chapter fifteen

Cooper and Belle were enjoying the Saturday morning sunshine from the backyard deck when Lucy finally poked her head out, "Good morning."

"Good morning. What time did you get in last night? I didn't hear a thing."

"Late. Very late. After dinner and the movie, we ended up in Melbourne Street at one of those places which sell late night coffee and dessert. We talked for hours and hours. It's amazing how you think you know a person because you see them every week but when you actually talk to them, you find out so much more than you ever expected."

Belle hid a faint grin at this 'waxing lyrical' and did the nice sisterly thing by asking, "What did you find out?"

Lucy took a long drink of her coffee before replying, "He's really into extreme sports. The more extreme, the better. Sports is his main thing, both watching and playing them."

"You can't have talked about sports for all that time though. Did you tell him that your favourite exercise is shuffling those tarot cards?"

"Hey, I exercise; sometimes. But we talked about lots of things; work, our families; our childhoods; where we've travelled and where we want to go. He spoke about work quite a bit actually. His friends tease him because he is "just" a delivery person. When he left school, Noah started at Adelaide University studying science intending to work with the environment but after a year or so he was sick of all the arguing and back stabbing that goes on behind the scenes so he quit and now does volunteer work as well as his job. He figures he can do more good that way."

"He might be right," Belle didn't sound convinced but knew from past experiences that Lucy wouldn't hear anything bad about Noah at this point.

"He talked about our office too. How everyone except Arthur seemed to be nice enough although he did think that Jane could be too bossy with me sometimes. He said that because his work colleagues drive by themselves all day, it was hard to feel that "team" thing we seem to have going."

"What did he say about Arthur?" Belle was still looking for more 'Arthur related' ammunition.

"Apparently, Arthur treats him pretty much the way that Arthur treats all of us; like his servant. Noah was dropping off some paper this week and they got into a dance at the elevator doors. Noah was coming out of the lift with a hand trolley full of boxes of paper and Arthur was annoyed that he had to wait, especially because he was on his way out for lunch, so he voiced his unhappiness, just like he does with all of us."

"Nothing new there then," Belle sighed, "Where does he volunteer?"

"He works with an organisation called Trees for Life which tries to preserve and regenerate our land especially after natural disasters like last year's bushfires. He seems to be pretty hands on, weeding, planting trees and such.

"Good on him. It's always nice to hear of someone who lives up to his principles."

"Yeah it is. Did you know that he grew up in the next suburb from us? But apart from location, our childhoods were very different. His dad died when Noah was five and from what Noah didn't say, I'm guessing he wasn't a very nice man before that. Perhaps that explains why he is so fiercely protective of his mum and younger sister."

"Younger sister?"

"Yes, he has one younger sister. She's married with two small kids, three and five. I think he spends quite a bit of time with his niece and nephew. Apparently, they all love going to the football, to see both the men's and women's teams and are huge Crows fans."

"What's going to happen when you tell him that you hate football? I'm assuming you just smiled and nodded last night."

"It will work out. He can keep going to the football with the kids or his friends and we can do other things together."

"So, you're going to see him again?"

Lucy blushed, "I hope so. Nothing was arranged but he said he'd see me at work this week so maybe he'll ask me to have lunch again."

"You could always ask him?"

"After Kaili; no. I want someone who is prepared to put in some effort. If he wants to see me again, he has to ask," then Lucy laughed, "But I gave him my mobile number, my work number, my home email and my work email so I made sure he could find me."

Belle shook her head, picking up her coffee cup and starting inside, "It sounds like you had a lovely time and I'm sure he'll be in touch very soon."

Belle looked back from the doorway and said, "Once you've finished your coffee, let's go to Jane's and get this search over because we need to think about dinner with Georgie and Oliver."

Lucy mumbled her agreement as Cooper followed Belle inside hoping for a snack.

chapter sixteen

The twin's first impression of Jane's home was of a fairly moderntype house with clean lines and a manicured front yard set in a neighbourhood of heritage family homes with wild overflowing gardens. Jane's address, obtained from the Employee Contact Details held on file at work, did not indicate such a contrast from the neighbouring properties.

As the twins entered the property, the first thing they did was to empty the letterbox of a few random flyers and two supermarket advertising brochures. It had only been four days since Jane's demise but the twins were surprised at the lack of actual mail in the letterbox.

As Lucy flicked through the contents she remarked, "Can you remember when we would get something in the post every day? A bill or a letter or a reminder? Now it's unusual for the postie to stop at our house."

She continued, "But that's normal for us because all of our bills and reminders and everything else are sent online now. So, around our birthday and Christmas are the only times we expect to get stuff in the letterbox. But I'm surprised that Jane doesn't have more letters; do you think she got her bills online too? I didn't think she was that tech savvy."

"Ummm," Belle was trying the different keys to find one to open the screen door, "No-one has mentioned an alarm system, so I hope she doesn't ... didn't have one."

As Belle entered Jane's home, she came to an abrupt stop. The inside décor was so different to the exterior. The curtains were closed so the only light came from the opened door but it was enough to see the surprising interior. Inside was like a typical old English woman's front parlour. Every spare inch of space was occupied; by heavy, dark, wooden furniture, by old-fashioned doodads; by framed pictures, not of people, but of cat posters and embroidered sayings. Each step the twins took risked knocking something over.

"Holy hell," gaped Lucy putting the box of Jane's personal belongings on the floor, "How did the police search this place? It looks like an old-time movie set."

"Yeah who knows if anything is out of place. I'm wondering if they're concentrating on the work aspect until something indicates her home life played a part in her murder. This place is too much."

"Where are we going to start then?" asked Lucy, "We at least have to try and find the expo permits."

Belle looked around the room then walked towards one of the bedrooms. The house consisted of two bedrooms, a combined lounge, kitchen and dining room plus the wet areas.

"You look out here in the combined rooms and I'll tackle the bedrooms. It looks like she used the second bedroom as an office so I'll start there."

The twins started their search with trepidation but after a few minutes of gingerly picking up things and shaking them to see if anything fell out, they began rifling with more gusto. Belle quickly found the expo permits lying openly on Jane's desk but was more interested in what she found stacked neatly in the bookcase.

It seemed like Jane was an amateur entrepreneur or maybe just a gambler of sorts. One entire shelf of her office bookcase was dedicated to books about how to profit from the share market. There must have been fifteen different books with flashy titles aimed at making money.

Also on the bookcase were two different piles, one of losing instant scratchie tickets and the other of TAB betting slips. The $5 scratchie tickets all had a month and year written on them and the tickets, about twenty, were in month order. There were more betting slips, maybe fifty, and they were a mixture of winning bets and losing wagers. They were mainly win/place bets of no more than $10 per slip and grouped in date order as well.

Belle looked at the share market books again and sure enough, at the end there were four books with titles relating to horse racing and how to make money from betting.

It looked like Jane was really interested in making some extra money.

There was a laptop on the desk which Belle decided to leave for Lucy to investigate; Lucy was definitely more technologically minded than she was.

"Lucy, did you find anything?"

Lucy walked into the office, "We'll need to clean the fridge out before we leave and Jane ate a lot of chocolate but no, nothing of any note. That's probably why the police let Jennifer have access to it so quickly."

"Well I found something. Look."

Belle showed Lucy the gambling books, the losing tickets and the rest of Jane's betting collection, "And she has a laptop here, can you get into it?"

"Depends on whether she had a password or not," Lucy opened up the laptop.

Stuck to the screen was a sticky note with the letters 'lasvegashereicome'. Lucy looked at Belle, "Surely she wasn't that dumb. Not after all the office training we've had on computer security."

Lucy turned the laptop on and when the password question appeared, she entered the letters from the sticky note and sure enough, that gave access to the computer and the desktop background showed a stunning picture of the Las Vegas Strip at night with all the sparkling lights from the many casinos.

"I'm thinking that Las Vegas and gambling was rather important to Jane," Lucy mused.

"Important or an obsession?" replied Belle, "Any why did she never talk about it at work? It's a lot more interesting that those boring stories about her latest knitting project."

"Hey, I like knitting," Lucy said, "But we were right, she wasn't that tech savvy. It doesn't look like she used the laptop for anything but a couple of spreadsheets. I can't even find any evidence of email on here."

"So, what is on there?"

"There are four spreadsheets, each one named something specific; Las Vegas, Horse Racing, Scratchies and Shares."

Lucy opened the Las Vegas spreadsheet and everything became clearer. Jane was clearly working towards a lavish holiday in Las Vegas. There were details of her goal; a first class return airline ticket costing around $20,000, 14 nights in a Bellagio King Room at $400 per night plus gambling money and miscellaneous expenses altogether totalling $40,000.

From the spreadsheet, it appeared that Jane was well over halfway to her Las Vegas goal but there was no sign where the money was.

Lucy closed that spreadsheet and opened the one titled Shares. This spreadsheet contained a record of all the shares Jane had bought and sold, the capital gains and losses plus all the dividends she'd received. From the separate sheets for each financial year, Jane had been playing the stock market for at least five years.

The next spreadsheet wasn't as interesting. It detailed all the scratchies Jane had purchased, where they'd been bought and any winnings. Looking at where the scratchies had been bought, it showed a pattern of Jane's preferred places and strangely how some places just did not provide winning tickets.

The last spreadsheet was titled Horse Racing. Again, it was a detailed list of Jane's gambling habits, this time related to horse racing. It listed the horses Jane had backed, how much she'd staked plus the wins and losses. There was also information on the associated trainers and jockeys.

"I'm surprised there weren't more losing scratchies and betting tickets," Lucy mused, "These spreadsheets have data going back several years but all the ones we found were quite recent."

Belle started looking for further evidence of a prolonged gambling habit and there at the bottom of Jane's wardrobe were many more boxes of tickets and scratchies. The ones on the bookcase were only for the last month and there was definitely evidence of an ongoing problem.

"This is all very interesting but what, if anything, does it have to do with her murder?" asked Lucy.

"Maybe she used information from the wrong person to make her bets or sell her shares? Like she overheard Mark talking about his stock market stuff and used it for her own good and Mark found out and he killed her. Or Jane was blackmailing Mark to get his stock market tips and he got sick of it and killed her."

"Or Jack sometimes talks about going to the races so maybe she used him to bet on a sure thing horse and the bookie who had to pay out all that money murdered her. Or Jack's contacts are mad that Jane found out about the sure thing horse and told Jack to kill her," Belle was on a roll and sensible logic had flown out of the window.

"And how did these bookies get in the office to kill her?" Lucy rolled her eyes at Belle, "I think you need some food."

"But at least we have a couple of new leads we can follow up," said Belle, "And we need to talk to Jennifer again and see if she knew about that extra money and where it might be."

"Yeah, $20,000 is a pretty good motive for anyone."

chapter seventeen

The twins stopped at the shops on the way home from Jane's house and picked up lunch plus a freshly homemade vegetarian lasagne with crunchy rolls for dinner. After eating lunch, Lucy made their grandmother's old fashioned sultana cake for this evening's dessert. Oliver, Georgie's husband was very partial to this cake which was made with a lot of butter, sugar and sultanas and had mashed pumpkin as the secret ingredient.

While Lucy was making the cake, Belle whipped up a green salad to go with the lasagne and quickly tidied the house. Their home would never be fit for the queen but it was warm and welcoming. Cooper, meanwhile, relaxed in the sunshine and paid no heed to all this activity.

Georgie and Oliver arrived just as the kitchen clock clicked over to 7.00pm and Belle put the lasagne in the oven. Oliver was holding a nice bottle of red wine while Georgie offered Lucy a scrumptious looking cheese platter as she greeted them at the front door.

"This looks nice," Lucy commented as she accepted the cheese platter and ushered their guests into the loungeroom.

Belle joined them asking, "I've just put dinner in the oven to heat and it will be about 45 minutes; can I get everyone a drink while we wait?"

Lucy put the cheese platter on the coffee table as Belle took the drink orders. Once they were all settled with their drinks and had chosen from the cheese platter, Georgie asked, "What have you found out? I have so much to tell you."

"It's hard to believe that Jane was only killed three days ago," Lucy started. She continued to summarise everything they had discovered since Tuesday's dinner.

She spoke about everyone's alibis, the motives they had uncovered and those still unclear. She told Georgie and Oliver about Frank's refusal to say where he was and how Kelly was quick to gossip about others in the office while keeping quiet about her own motive. Lucy covered Arthur's daughter wanting to join the police force, the niggling between Jane and Kevin and then how Paige had given two different version of events.

Lucy finished with the results of today's search of Jane's home, "Jane was a gambler. We found all these betting records in her house. She liked horse racing, the stock market and scratchies."

Oliver smiled, "Scratchies are a good money waster but you're not going to win big with them."

"You never know, you might win the big prize," Lucy retorted.

"I love my scratchies and the most I've ever won is $40.00 and that was years ago. I'm sure they have just enough small prizes to keep people coming back,"

Belle interrupted, "I've never really played scratchies, how do they work?"

"Well, you buy the scratchie ticket, get a coin and scratch the ticket. If you have the right combination, you win. If you don't, you lose," Oliver deadpanned.

Belle laughed, "I know that much, I'm asking because Jane had written a month on each of the losing tickets and I was wondering if you knew why she would do this."

"What denominations were the tickets? $2.00, $5.00 ... "

"They were predominantly Crossword scratchie tickets, I think they were $5.00, why?

"The Lottery Commission runs a Second Chance Draw for some of losing scratchies. You can submit the code for any of your losing tickets and once a month, they run another draw. But you do need to keep your losing tickets in case you win. Jane probably was noting what month she had submitted each ticket for this Second Chance Draw."

"You certainly know a lot about scratchies ..." commented Belle with a wink.

"I know all about his scratchie addiction," Georgie laughed, "Maybe one day he'll win the jackpot."

"Hey, the Second Chance Draw is worth $10,000. I'd be happy with that."

"I'm just happy that scratchies and the occasional lotto ticket are the extent of his gambling," Georgie said as she reached for another piece of cheese with a biscuit.

"Jane was into a lot more than just scratchies," said Lucy as she too took a biscuit from the platter, "From her records, most of her gambling was on the stock market during the week and then horseracing on Saturday. Scratchies were just a sideline."

"But what does that have to do with her murder?" asked Georgie.

"Don't know. Maybe nothing. But also, maybe something. Mark is heavily invested in the stock market and Jack has some connection to horse racing so this brings the possibility of other motives that we had no idea about."

Belle interrupted again, "And don't forget Jennifer."

"Who's Jennifer?"

"Jane's daughter. She's the beneficiary of Jane's will and there seems to be quite a bit of money around somewhere. She has an alibi but we've decided to check a bit further now all this money is involved and she was so cold. Surely even if you were estranged from your mother, you would express some sadness if she was killed."

Georgie and Oliver looked confused so Lucy belatedly explained what they'd found about Jane's daughter.

The oven timer interrupted and Belle left to serve dinner as the rest of the group moved to the dining table with their drinks. Lucy topped up those drinks and by unspoken agreement, the conversation over dinner focussed on other parts of their lives.

Lucy spoke about her date with Noah, then having forgotten that Georgie didn't know about the break-up with Kaili, she had to explain that too. Oliver spoke about his crazy work schedule and told the story of a customer who answered the door in a see-through negligee. Apparently, she was trying to make her husband jealous and thought a dalliance with the electrician would suffice. She was rather disappointed when Oliver declined. Georgie and Belle exchanged dog stories and a lovely dinner was had by all.

chapter eighteen

After dinner, Lucy made coffee and the group settled back in the loungeroom with the delicious sultana cake and the rest of the cheese platter. Georgie pulled her notes from her handbag, "Let me tell you what I found out online."

"I checked Facebook, Instagram, Twitter and then looked for any other online presence. I also thought about Snapchat but with the messages disappearing after a few seconds I decided it would be a waste of time." Georgie started, "You were right about Arthur, he had nothing online. No social media of any sort and when I googled his name, nothing came up either. Jane was similar, she had a Facebook page but there were only a few posts about the CWA cooking competitions. She either didn't access it or only used it to look at other people's posts."

"Facebook was where I found out the most information. Arthur was the only one who didn't have a Facebook page. But there was a lot of difference in how much your individual colleagues used it."

"Interestingly, none of them had their privacy controls set up," Georgie continued, "And after this you really need to talk to Kelly about it. She is always posting pictures of her kids and everyone can see them."

"I'll talk to her," Belle grimaced, "After all the work training we get on privacy and the importance of the different settings, you think these people would know better."

"And mention her Instagram account too, she seems to post the same kids pictures on both and her Instagram is a public account too. But I never saw a Story from her on either platform."

Belle shook her head, "Was there anything unusual in her postings?"

"No. They were all pictures of the family, doing family things like washing the car, picnicking on the beach and so on. But it certainly showed how important her family is to her. If Jane did or said something to threaten it, that could be a motive for Kelly. I have no doubt Kelly would protect her family to the very end."

"Except when it comes to privacy settings," Oliver quipped.

"Anything else?"

"No. Kelly only had Facebook and Instagram, no Twitter and nothing general on line."

Georgie shuffled her notes, "Now Mark is a different story. He has Facebook, Instagram, Twitter and a LinkedIn profile. Is he married? Does he have kids?"

"Not anymore. Well he's divorced and although he has two daughters, he doesn't mention them at all and there's no photos of them in his office so I don't think he has much to do with them. Why?" Lucy replied.

"I just wondered because his online presence was sad. Everything seems business related. Facebook only has the odd post but they're all about his business successes. Or what I'm guessing he thinks is a success."

"Like what?"

"Posts about making money, promotions, new company cars, bigger office. But there's never any people in these photos. And like Kelly, his Instagram account is just a copy of his Facebook page. Twitter is different, but again it's all about business. He rants about how the government is hampering the small stock market investor by the rules which apply and how to get around them. And if he's cheating the Tax Department, he's certainly not smart because anybody could read his methods. And 'anybody' could include Jane which would give her ample blackmail material."

"He really tweeted how to cheat the tax department?" Belle was astonished.

"It's not as exact as that but if you look at his history, patterns of suggested behaviour emerge which are shady and there was one post on Facebook which has more detail. And if Jane wanted money that badly, she might have thought the research worth her while. She might even have been cheating the Tax Department herself."

Belle looked at Lucy, "We should have taken her laptop when we had the chance."

"Maybe we should go back tomorrow and take it. Jennifer did say we could take what we like. And if we have time, we could speak to her neighbours and see if they know anything?"

Oliver was scrapping his plate for every last crumb of the cake, Lucy laughed and took the plate from him, "Would anyone else like another piece of cake, or more coffee?"

Once they'd all been replenished, Belle asked, "What did you find on Jack?"

"He definitely has something to do with horse racing. A lot of his posts are when he's at the racetrack. And there are even posts with horses that seem to be at someone's stables."

"As well as that, there are lots of posts on Facebook about sports and him playing or watching them. I really don't know why people have both Facebook and Instagram, he's another one that posts exactly the same thing on both platforms."

"Anything else?" Belle asked.

"Like Mark, he has a LinkedIn profile and he seems to be pretty serious about his career and where he wants to end up. Did you know he's considering running for political office?"

"No, but we mainly talk about work stuff," replied Belle, "I wonder if that's why he always wants to keep the peace? Doesn't want to make enemies if he does run for something."

"That's the problem with social media," said Oliver, "People generally only put up the best version of themselves and even if it's a bad photo or a stupid mistake, people post them in a way that's self-deprecating so others feel empathy with them."

"I don't agree," Lucy replied, "Some people use their social media platforms to highlight important things, not just pictures of themselves. Noah and I were comparing our Facebook pages last night and his is either about bullying or the environment and all the different resources that are available these days for both."

"The environment I understand with his volunteering but why is Noah interested in bullying?" Belle asked.

"I gather it's something to do with his Dad. He just said that no-one he loved would ever be bullied again and he was doing all he could to raise its profile. But it shows that social media can be used for more than just selfies."

Belle laughed, "Can you imagine Frank or Kevin posting selfies?"

"You might be surprised, both of them have Facebook pages and use them," Georgie said, "Frank more so than Kevin and he's obviously obsessed with football. All of his posts have something to do with the AFL or some other football related thing. But neither have Instagram accounts or anything else online."

"Are any of Frank's Facebook posts about the AFLW?" Lucy asked, "I can't see him being a fan of the women invading his space."

"No, nothing to do with the AFLW, either good or bad. But his name was mentioned in a few articles when I did a general internet search. All related to him refereeing football games."

"And what about Kevin?"

"He doesn't post as often as Frank but his tastes are definitely wider. His posts are quite strange really."

"In what way?"

"From what you told me, he's a gamer of sorts, and technical. He doesn't post about either of these interests. He seems to like auctions and these range from Ebay to Christies Auction House. He regularly posts on items he's interested in and no two items seem the same. I've seen posts on Star Wars figurines and antique clocks."

Belle shrugged her shoulders, "It is strange but harmless I suppose unless you found anything else?

"No, nothing else but I might dig a bit further," replied Georgie, "And last of the suspects is Paige. She is the one with the most social media activity. She has Facebook, Instagram and Twitter. Although again I don't know why she has Twitter, everything comes from either her Facebook or Instagram."

"Must be an age thing."

"Well she posts on Facebook most days and lots of pictures of the food she eaten."

"I've never understood this," interrupted Oliver, "Why would you let your meal go cold or get hot just to get a photo of it to post somewhere? Why not just eat and enjoy the food?"

Georgie laughed, "Not everyone is as food obsessed as you. Anyway, Facebook gets all the food photos while Instagram has food shots as well but it's her stories which are interesting. I've been regularly looking at them over the last couple of days and she's been posting prophetic sayings like 'If you tell the truth, you don't have to remember anything.' And 'The truth is rarely pure and never simple.' Sounds to me like someone who has something to hide and is worried about it."

"That ties in with what Jules noticed from the spreadsheet," Belle said, "We really need to have a good chat with her on Monday morning."

"Thanks for this Georgie, you did great," Lucy smiled, "And could you please check out one more person? Jennifer Petras, she's Jane's daughter."

"Sure, I'll have a snoop tomorrow and give you a call. I assume her maiden name was King like her mother's?"

After a long night of talking and eating, Georgie and Oliver finished their drinks and started gathering their things to head home. Lucy dashed into the kitchen and cut a huge chunk of sultana cake for Oliver to take home with him.

"I'll get all of this information to Jules so she can add it to the spreadsheet," Lucy hugged Georgie, "I don't know how to thank you for all your hard work."

"Anything to keep you out of jail," Georgie joked.

Belle and Lucy exchanged worried glances, jail might become a reality if they didn't find something soon.

chapter nineteen

Sunday started slowly for the twins. They were due at their parents for lunch and wanted to go back to Jane's place afterwards but there was nothing urgent to get out of bed for.

Mid-morning, Belle took Cooper for a run at a nearby dog park while Lucy brought a cup of tea and the Sunday paper out to the back deck. It was nice to have a spell from the thoughts that had been plaguing them both; did they really know someone who was capable of killing another person and what would happen to Lucy if the police decided to proceed with the case and the evidence they had? Were they helping or hindering the police investigation? Or were they having no impact whatsoever? What if they were making things worse? A morning free of these troubling questions was just what they needed.

But unfortunately, all good things must eventually end. Lucy needed to get petrol so after filling up her tank she drove them both to their parent's house for lunch. Their Mum was rostered on in the Hospital's Emergency Room that day, so their Dad was in charge of the food. As a mother and a nurse, Laura was a firm believer in a balanced diet which included fruit and vegetables. Sam, on the other hand, was more of a meat only guy when given the choice. And with Sam preparing lunch today, it consisted of a basic BBQ with chops and sausages plus some chips to provide the vegetable part of the meal. Lucy brought some left-over sultana cake for dessert to round out the meal.

When everyone had a full plate and they were sitting at the dining table, Sam asked, "What's been happening with you two this week? Your Mum told me about that lady in your office."

"You remember Jane? She's the horrible one who sticks her nose in everywhere when it's not wanted? Somebody obviously had enough of her and clonked her on the head," Lucy made light of her horrific discovery. It had only been five days but it felt both a lot longer and also as if it was only yesterday that she'd found the body.

Lucy proceeded to give her Dad a detailed account of the past few days. She spoke about the shock of finding Jane, the body, the blood and all caused by the big stapler which everyone had used at some point in time. The sheer unluckiness of Jane dying from a single blow because of her own physical form. She spoke about the different reactions from her colleagues and how there was little grief in the office. She listed the different office suspects and how each of them had a motive to kill Jane; from the small motive of dislike to bigger motives relating to money and reputations.

Lucy pondered the life of someone who was universally disliked and noted how they hadn't found anyone with something good to say about Jane or who admitted that they would miss her. And this ranged from her office workmates to her only daughter. From Jane's daughter, she moved on to considering Arthur's daughter and the sadness that families can generate. And how a person could be living a secret life to the oblivion of those around them. Who knew that Arthur was intent on hindering his daughter's choices or that Jane was an amateur gambler?

Books always say that the character of the victim is all important and knowing how the victim lived often led to identifying their murderer. Lucy spoke about how she would not have included horse-racing, scratchies or shares in her previous knowledge of Jane the office co-worker in a million years. She wondered what else she would find out.

In some ways, the conversation seemed cathartic until Lucy made the mistake of saying, "Sometimes when we are investigating, I forget she was an actual person."

"Investigating?" Sam queried, "What do you mean; investigating?"

"Umm … "Lucy faltered. She looked at her plate and picked up a lukewarm chip and slowly chewed on it.

"Dad," Belle said, "Lucy is the police's main suspect. Since she found the body after having a huge fight with Jane, the police think she killed her."

"That's ridiculous," exclaimed Sam.

"We know that but while the police think Lucy did it, they're not looking any further so we decided to ask a few questions."

"Why didn't you tell me?"

"We told Mum but I guess she decided not to tell you in case you threw a wobbly," Belle joked.

"Mmmm. I don't like being kept in the dark and I definitely don't like you girls being in danger. If a person has killed once, the experts always say the next kill is easier."

"We're just asking a few questions and if we find anything important we'll tell the police. Charlie will help; even though, like you, she is not happy with us doing this," said Lucy.

"Surprisingly, I'm quite liking the puzzle aspect of this," Belle admitted, "And I love our spreadsheet."

"Spreadsheet?" asked Sam.

Belle explained the spreadsheet they were keeping; all the suspects, the motives and their alibis, "It's good to see all the information we've collected in one place. And Jules is pretty good at looking at all the data and seeing patterns where you might not notice if you're just talking about it."

"It does look like you have it well organised. And as long as you're not taking any chances with your safety," Sam grudgingly conceded as he picked up the empty plates and took them to the kitchen, "Is there anything I can do to help you?"

Belle and Lucy glanced at each other before shaking their heads.

"At least think about moving here for the duration," Sam insisted, "I would feel a lot better if I knew you were safe each night."

Like any good parent, Sam knew his daughters needed to be independent. He and Laura had taught them to stand tall, to fend for themselves and care for others but that didn't mean he had to like it when they put the teachings into practice. Especially when murder was on the table.

Belle smiled, "Thanks for the offer but we're safe at our home. Coop will let us know if anything is amiss."

"Cooper?" Sam laughed, "Cooper is a useless guard dog. The only way he'd help you is if your attackers rang the doorbell."

Lucy laughed while Belle protested. Sam put his arm around Belle, "Let's have some coffee and sultana cake before you girls leave and I can sit on the couch for an afternoon of golf on the TV."

chapter twenty

As the twins once again opened the door to Jane's house, they experienced a feeling of being watched. Belle looked around and saw an old woman, maybe in her eighties, peering out from her curtain in the house across the road.

"We should go and talk to her," Belle said, "She looks like the neighbourhood gossip, keeping an eye on everything from behind her curtains."

"Sure, let's get the laptop then go over there."

The twins entered the house with a feeling of unease, even though they had the key and permission to take whatever they needed, it felt slightly wrong to be back here again without anyone knowing.

As they walked through the loungeroom, Belle noticed that things were not quite where they were last time. The fine layer of dust on the furniture showed the photo frames had been moved, just a fraction. It was like someone had come here and had a look around since yesterday. Nothing was obviously missing, although it would be hard to be certain with all the doodads.

"Look at this," Belle exclaimed, "These things have been moved. Somebody has been here after we left yesterday afternoon."

"Let's get out of here, it's creepy," replied Lucy, shifting her glance from side to side.

"Whoever was here is not anymore," Belle muttered while looking around the room but could see no clear signs of a search, "I wonder who it was. The obvious person is her landlord just being nosy but maybe Jane had something the murderer wanted and they needed to get it back."

"How would the murderer get in? Only us, the police and the landlord have keys."

"Unless they broke in? Should we check?"

"It was probably the police, that would explain why there doesn't seem to be anything missing."

"Except the police released it as a crime scene before we came in yesterday. Why would they need to come back again?"

Belle went and checked the back door and pulled the curtains aside to make certain the windows were all still intact. Everything seemed to be as it should.

They quickly gathered up the laptop and a couple of external hard drives from the office bookcase. As they closed and locked the front door, Belle looked across at the old neighbour still staring at them, "Let's go talk to her, maybe she knows who else has come to Jane's place."

Lucy and Belle crossed the road and walked up the driveway where the elderly woman was still peering out from behind the curtain. Her front yard was manicured to perfection. There were no weeds to be seen, the grass was cut to a standard height across the lawn and the plants were blooming or ready to start. This was obviously a garden that was well tended.

Lucy rang the doorbell and the twins waited patiently for the door to be opened. After a little while, the door opened a crack and a surprisingly strong voice asked, "How can I help you?"

"Hi, we're work colleagues of Jane, from across the road, and were wondering if we could ask you a couple of questions?"

"Why should I talk to you? The police came and saw me earlier in the week and I told them everything I know."

"We might ask you different things and we can tell you what we know too," Lucy cajoled, thinking that any gossip would surely like to know what was going on.

"That's a good point," she said opening the door up wider, "But you're not coming inside. You hear all those scams about young people taking advantage of older people."

"No problem, we can talk out here," said Lucy, "I'm Lucy Anderson and this is my sister, Belle. We worked with Jane and are … umm … looking into Jane's death."

"My name is Margaret Gale. I've lived here for nearly fifty years, first with my late husband and then by myself when he passed on."

The twins murmured their condolences.

"It was a long time ago and now I spend my days out in the garden or sitting on the lounge with a nice big crossword."

"Do you like to knit?" Lucy asked.

"What? You think because I'm older, I should be tucked up with a blanket around my knees, knitting bootees for my great grandchildren?"

"No," Lucy replied rather flustered at the outraged tone of Margaret's response, "I like knitting but Belle hates it so I was thinking that if you liked it, we might be able to compare our projects and have something in common."

"Humfp. Then no, I don't like knitting."

Belle interrupted and asked about Margaret's time in the garden, "You have a clear view from your yard to Jane's front door, have you ever seen anybody go into her house?"

"You tell me what you know first, then I'll tell you what I've seen."

Belle told of Lucy finding the body, said a little about what the police had informed Mark and asked again, "Who have you seen going into Jane's house?"

Margaret looked thoughtfully at the twins, "Nobody."

"Nobody?"

"Except for the police last week and you two yesterday, I've never seen anybody go into that house in the whole time I've lived here."

"Jane was an odd duck," Margaret continued, "She kept to herself to the extent of no-one really knowing her. I only ever saw her going to and from what I assumed was work. She was dressed for working in an office but didn't wear a uniform."

"She worked at the council offices with us," Lucy replied to the unasked question.

"In the whole time we were neighbours, I only went inside her front door once. I was in the middle of making a big Mother's Day Sunday lunch for my entire family and I ran out of sugar. Cliched I know, but none of my other neighbours were home so I took a chance and knocked on her door. Thankfully she was home and let me in. While she was filling my container with sugar I looked around, as you do, and I was saddened to see nothing. It was Mother's Day and there were no flowers or cards, no lunchtime preparations, only the computer lit up in the little room off the lounge; the house had a slightly neglected feel about it. I remember feeling very sad for her and very grateful for my large, noisy family which was about to descend on me. Did she have any children?"

"One daughter but they were estranged," answered Lucy, "And you never saw anyone else there?"

"It was like a force field surrounded the house, no-one ventured up the driveway. I've even seen both charity collectors and Jehovah Witnesses avoid that property. And while the garden lacks the character of most of the houses around here, the landlord did a pretty good job of keeping the front yard cleaned and tidy."

"So, the landlord came onto the property regularly?

"Yes, he came about once a month to mow the lawn and weed the garden, such as it is."

"Was yesterday the first time you saw him go into the house?" Belle took a small gamble.

"Yes, you're right. Normally he would just be outside but yesterday he went in for about an hour or so. I wonder what he was doing? I'd forgotten that he went inside."

The twins glanced at each other.

"Did you know him well? What sort of person was he?"

"I only knew him by sight, never spoken to the man."

"What about Jane, did you have much to do with her?" asked Lucy.

"Not really, we'd wave at each other if I was out in the garden when she was going somewhere. She only seemed to go to work and sometimes I would see her bringing shopping bags home. Except for that, she spent her time inside her house. But she did keep strange hours sometimes."

"What do you mean?"

"I'm old," Margaret stated bluntly, "And I get up to go to the bathroom quite regularly during the night. There were many nights when I would be awake in the wee hours and Jane's lights would be on plus there would be flickering lights like the TV or her computer in the background. I always thought she must have been an insomniac."

Lucy glanced at Belle who shrugged her shoulders, "What would you say if we told you we found lots of evidence that Jane was a gambler?"

Margaret considered this, "I wouldn't be totally surprised. I've always thought that people who gamble are lonely and missing something in their lives. That would fit with my impression of Jane. And especially if she was gambling using her computer, that would fit with the unusual lights flickering at night."

"But, how well do we really know anyone? Doesn't everyone have something to hide?" and with this, Margaret closed her front door.

chapter twenty-one

Later that night, the twins were finishing their dinner when the phone rang. It was Georgie reporting back what she'd found with Jennifer's social media so Belle put it on speakerphone. Georgie had found both Facebook and Instagram accounts for Jennifer with mainly photos of her family. She seemed to be a happy woman in a group of friends with kids and the photos showed them all doing kids crafty things, like painting and play doh sculpting. Occasionally the husbands appeared but these posts were more BBQ type events. There was nothing that screamed 'killer'.

"Thanks Georgie, we'll see you for dinner on Tuesday," Belle hung up the phone.

"I suppose we shouldn't be surprised," commented Lucy. "If someone was going to kill their mother, they'd hardly announce it on Facebook."

Belle laughed, "No, I guess not."

"And Margaret didn't help much either, did she?"

"There wasn't much new information but she did confirm a couple of things about Jane; like her being standoffish and not being part of the neighbourhood. And she did agree that the gambling might be possible."

"And she said the landlord went inside yesterday so he's probably the one who shifted her things in the loungeroom. But why?"

"It could be as simple as him being nosy or he could have been looking for something. And if it was looking for something specific, that opens things up for another suspect."

"But we still have the problem of how did anyone else get into the photocopier room? You need a pass key."

"What if we've been looking at this all wrong? What if someone came to the counter and Jane let them into the office? That means the killer could be someone we don't know. And it could be to do with her gambling or something else."

Lucy thought about this scenario, "This is both good news and bad news. The good news is that the killer might not be someone we know and work with every day but the bad news is that it could be anyone now."

Their task seemed to be developing into a mammoth undertaking.

****

Monday started well with the sun shining, no traffic and easy parking for both of the twins as they started their day, all be it at different times. Things disintegrated from there.

First person in the office, Belle was greeted by a stack of emails asking about the Pet Expo and all wanting an immediate response. It looked like panic had started over the weekend and her day would be spent reassuring everyone from suppliers, to demonstrators, to the winners of the competitions.

When Lucy arrived about an hour later, she was greeted by a patiently waiting Sergeant Harris.

"Could I please have a few minutes of your time?" he asked.

"Of course," Lucy replied, "Let's go and see if anyone's in the conference room."

Before leaving the office, Lucy quickly asked Kelly to keep an eye on the front desk. Then as Lucy and Sgt Harris walked down the hall to the conference room, Paige was coming towards them and turned grey at the sight of the police officer. Lucy turned her head as they passed each other and wondered at the extreme reaction.

The conference room was empty so Lucy closed the door and she and Sergeant Harris took seats on opposite sides of the table. Lucy sat silently waiting for him to begin.

"I know there was some indication that you were considered the chief suspect because of the hostile relationship between you and the deceased. However, the victim appears to have had hostile relationships with everybody both in this office and in her personal life. Based on that new information we have been investigating further and several other suspects have emerged."

"Are you saying I'm no longer the main villain in this story?" Lucy asked sarcastically.

"Yes. You are no longer a person of interest. However, there is still one small thing which I'd like clarified. There is an avenue of time for which you have not accounted for your whereabouts. Where were you between 11.30am and 12.00pm?"

"I told you, I was downstairs getting the mail. That's why no-one saw me, I was downstairs. Then when I got back Mark had left all these envelopes for me to deliver. I did think it was strange that he wanted the envelopes delivered immediately but he's the boss so I just did what he asked."

"You were seen while delivering the envelopes but we have been told that you are normally absent from the office each day for approximately fifteen minutes when collecting the mail. This leaves fifteen minutes unaccounted for within the critical timeframe where no-one saw you. Did you do something else?"

Lucy thought back, "I know I left at exactly 11.30am to get the mail because I was running late and definitely wanted to be back by 12.00pm in case Noah asked me to lunch again."

"Noah?"

"Our stationery delivery person. We'd had lunch on the day before and I was hoping that he would ask me again. You see he normally delivers to the council offices on Mondays and Tuesdays but it doesn't matter now because we had dinner on Friday night and I'm hoping I'll see him today. He did ask if I could see him over the weekend but I'd already made plans with Belle, and Georgie and Oliver plus Dad on Sunday so we decided to catch up this week."

Sergeant Harris was sitting there with a partially hidden grin. This was very different from her first interview, apparently to get Lucy to talk all you had to say was she'd been cleared, "You left your desk at 11.30am and went downstairs, collected the mail and then what? Did you see anyone? Do anything different? Go to the bathroom?"

Lucy racked her brain and suddenly exclaimed, "Yes!"

"Did you go to the bathroom? Who did you see?"

"No. As I was picking up the mail, Rachel was trying to carry all these boxes at once and nearly dropped the top one. I asked her if she needed a hand and I ended up carrying half of the boxes to her car. I remember being worried that I wouldn't get back before 12.00pm but I did. That's what took the extra time."

"Rachel …?"

"Rachel Donner, she works in the library downstairs. I'll ask her to give you a call."

"No, I'll contact her myself," said Sergeant Harris, making a note of her name.

"Is that it?" asked Lucy, "Can I go now?"

"Yes, you can go. I'll confirm this new information with Ms Donner and then I'll be able to cross you off my list as a suspect."

Lucy smiled in relief, "That is so good to know, now we can stop looking into what happened."

"You've been doing what?" Sergeant Harris did not seem impressed.

"I knew I hadn't killed her and you weren't investigating anyone else, so we decided to ask a few questions."

Sergeant Harris shook his head, "Keep out of it. It is not your job and with a killer still on the loose, it might be dangerous."

"Fine."

As Lucy was leaving, she turned and asked, "Do you want to know what we found out?"

"No thank you." Sergeant Harris kept his glance averted, "But could you please ask Paige Raynor to come and see me."

"Sure."

Lucy returned to the office and found Paige, "Sergeant Harris wants to see you. He's in the conference room."

Paige went a deathly shade of white and Lucy, afraid she was going to faint, quickly pushed her into a nearby chair. This was becoming a regular occurrence.

"Why does he want to see me?"

"He didn't say."

Paige hung her head, thinking furiously, "Will you come with me? And tell him I'm not a killer."

"I can certainly come with you," Lucy said tentatively, "And I know you relieved me at the front desk when I went to lunch. I can tell him that."

"Thanks."

Lucy and Paige walked to the conference room with Paige's steps becoming smaller and slower the closer they got. When they entered the room and Sergeant Harris looked up his first words were directed at Lucy, "Why are you back here?"

"Paige asked me to come with her and I thought we were told originally that we could have a support person with us during questioning if we wanted?"

"Okay, but your role is to quietly support Paige, not answer for her."

Lucy nodded and sat down in a vacant chair while Sergeant Harris turned towards Paige, "Thank you for coming, I've just got a couple of discrepancies I need to check."

Paige nodded.

"In your original and second statements, you said that you were in the office all morning, had an early lunch at your desk then covered the front desk when Lucy went to lunch."

"Yes, that's right."

"I'm sure you've heard that the hours we are concentrating on are between 11.30am and 2.00pm?"

"Yeah, I've heard."

"During our questioning, we can find no-one who can corroborate your statement."

"Lucy can," Paige interrupted, "Lucy, tell him that you saw me."

Lucy looked at Sgt Harris, "I saw Paige at 1.00pm when she relieved me at the front desk and I went to lunch. And I'm sure I would have heard if the front desk wasn't manned during my break."

"Did you see her at any time prior to that?"

"No."

Sgt Harris looked at Paige, "That covers part of the time. Can you remember talking to anyone else in the earlier period?"

"No," said Paige, "I was at my desk working. I was on a deadline and had my head down."

"Are you sure you didn't go outside for a quick break? We have information that you were seen in the carpark between 11.30am and 12.00pm."

Paige remained adamant that she hadn't left the office and refused to budge. Eventually Sgt Harris said she could go but that they would need to talk again later.

As Lucy and Paige walked down the corridor in silence, Lucy wondered if Paige was now Sgt Harris's main suspect in this drama. And if Sgt Harris was the right, was Lucy walking next to a killer?

chapter twenty-two

Belle's Monday morning email pile ran the gamut from Pet Expo suppliers, to contest entrants, to the exhibitors.

Her first task was to identify all the contest entrant's enquiries and tackle those. As the winners had been selected last Thursday by Mark, Jack and Lucy, it was now time to notify every one of the decisions and the next step from here. She checked her folder and found the list of entrants, the winners of both competitions plus the people selected as backups in case the winners were no longer interested or perhaps unable to take part.

Winners of the baking competition would be notified by email and asked to confirm their attendance. They would also be requested to submit their recipes including all required ingredients and equipment by the end of November. The council would provide everything they needed on the day. The email would also advise that details concerning where and when would be forwarded closer to the day of the Pet Expo.

As Belle was composing the generic email, it crossed her mind that the recipes submitted would need to be checked against the original entry, she added that to her list of things to do. Pressing the Send button on the final email, Belle smiled and muttered to herself, "One job done but I wonder how many will reply asking another question?"

Winners of the tasting competition would also be notified by email and asked to confirm their attendance and provide a scanned copy of the dog's current vaccination certificate. This time though they would be given instructions for their dogs such as bring them on a lead and feed them breakfast. As with the baking competition winners, the email would also advise that details concerning where and when would be forwarded closer to the day of the Pet Expo.

Belle's 'to do list' seemed to grow exponentially as she added 'arrange for water for the dogs' and 'ask sponsor to provide bowls for the tasting' after sending that bunch of emails.

The last group of competition emails were for those who were unsuccessful. Their email would thank them for entering and advise that unfortunately they hadn't been selected this time. It would invite them to attend the fair and include a voucher for a 20% discount from a pet treat exhibitor who was also one of the sponsors. Hopefully they would still come, even if they didn't win one of the competitions.

With both competitions on track, Belle decided to go and grab a cup of coffee. As she was waiting for the kettle to boil, Frank entered the kitchen.

"Hi Frank, how's things?" Belle asked.

"Okay I suppose," Frank replied, "It does seem quiet in the office without Jane. Who would've thought I'd miss her meddling?"

Jack joined them at the kettle, "Did you really say that you're missing Jane?"

"Weird, right?" Frank smiled.

"I don't know," Jack replied, "She was part of the council family, even if she was the grumpy aunt."

"Always tactful?" Belle baited, "Running for office, are you?"

"Not today," Jack smiled, "Do you know if Lucy found the food van permits that Jane was supposed to arrange?"

"Yeah we found them at her place over the weekend. Do you want them or should I just keep them with the rest of the paperwork?"

"You keep them. As long as I know we have them, I'm happy."

"The permits are fine and I found copies of the notifications to all the food and drink people advising that if they bring their trucks, the council will provide electricity and arrange for garbage collection, both during the event and at the close."

"Good job. And how's the rest going?"

"I've just finished emailing all the competition entrants, both winners and losers, and my next job is to check all the other paperwork and I need to get the resident's mailing list to Kelly so she can email out the advertising flyer," said Belle, "And Frank, how are you and Kevin progressing with the two dog guides? Will they be ready by Wednesday?"

"Should be," replied Frank, "I spoke to Paige on Friday and asked her to research some of the new options available for barking dogs as she's been

99

dealing with a lot of these complaints but I haven't seen her today. She's here or at least her computer is on."

"I saw her going to the conference room with Lucy," offered Jack, "And I saw Sgt Harris earlier this morning, so maybe she's being questioned again?"

Belle, knowing Lucy was planning on confronting Paige about her lying or at least misleading them about the murder, said, "Or perhaps they've just gotten caught up and Paige will be at her desk when you get back."

"Assuming Paige has her information ready, my guide will definitely be updated by Wednesday. You'll need to check with Kevin about his but he was working on it this morning."

"Okay, I'll ask him."

Belle left Jack and Frank in the kitchen with Frank refilling the kettle. As she returned to her desk, Belle's mind turned to Lucy and Paige. She wondered how Lucy was going. Had she found any useful information or was Paige still insisting that she hadn't left the office? Were they with Sgt Harris and if yes, what did that mean?

At her desk, Belle pulled out her phone and sent Lucy a quick text, just in case. Then she turned to her computer, accessed the Resident's Mailing List from Jane's files and sent it to Kelly with an instruction to send out the pre-approved flyer today if possible. Belle then ticked this job off her list as done, such was her faith in Kelly's reliability.

This set Belle thinking. If she had that much faith in Kelly, maybe it was time to take what she said as being right. And to assume that Kelly hadn't killed Jane. That would change the investigation. It would give them one less suspect and confirm possible motives for Arthur, Frank, Mark and Paige.

She shook her head, first things first. She must get this expo back on track then she could go back to thinking about murder suspects.

chapter twenty-three

The next job was to touch base with each of the exhibitors. The team had arranged for more than fifteen different exhibitors. There were pet stores and shops which supplied all manner of pet foods, accessories, treats even down to different poo bag options. A couple of dog training schools had wanted to be involved, it was a good way to advertise their services. And with what Belle considered a wonderful coup, there was even going to be a butcher's stand on the day. More and more people were feeding their dogs using a 'raw feed' model and getting their dog food from the butcher alongside their own meat.

Belle composed a form email to be sent to the exhibitors. The email included what the council would provide (tent, table and two chairs) and suggestions as to what the exhibitors should bring on the day. Pet shops needed to show what they had available for a wide range of animals including cats, mice, guinea pigs, snakes, rats, birds. Pet accessories businesses could show their wares for different pets too, such as leads, collars, bowls, harnesses and toys. Dog training schools were more limited in what pets they were focussing on but they could show different types of clickers, long leads, waist leads and even training treat bags. Pet food suppliers could again show what was available for all different pets including dry food, wet food, treats or organic food. Butchers while probably one of the most popular stands, would have a limited range of options available to them; raw feeding and bones, lots and lots of different size bones for different size dogs.

The emails also advised that details concerning where and when for each individual exhibitor would be forwarded closer to the day of the Pet Expo. As Belle pressed Send, she decided this would be a good excuse to have another chat with Arthur. Jack had placed him in charge of the Placement Map at the last meeting. Belle had been unhappy with this allocation of responsibilities as it decided where all the exhibitors would be located, where the final part of the competitions would take place plus of course placing toilets, electricity, water, poo bag stations and creating the right atmosphere with decorations and local musicians.

But as Jack hadn't listened to her, she just had to make the best of it and taking the opportunity for a chat with Arthur seemed fair. But the chat would have to wait until tomorrow; Arthur was enjoying a long weekend; or was he?

Belle skimmed over her emails, moving those she'd handled already and deleting others when she came across one she'd missed in her earlier scan. One of the vets scheduled to assist with the free microchipping of pets on the day had pulled out. Some nonsense about double booking and suddenly being unavailable. He was one of three vets scheduled for the day, perhaps they could manage with only two? Belle pulled out her phone and called Georgie.

"Hi, I have a disaster and need to ask your opinion," Belle exclaimed.

She explained the situation to Georgie who responded bluntly, "I told you right from the beginning that Dr Lewis was useless. Why didn't you ask us to send a vet?"

"I didn't want to take advantage because who knows if this is going to work."

"You'll definitely need three vets. Would you like me to ask here and see if someone is available on the day?"

"That would be wonderful. If there is one, they'll need to bring everything they need, drugs, certificates and the council will reimburse them afterwards."

"Are there going to be any vet nurses there to help?"

"I hadn't thought of that, what are you doing that day?" Belle quipped.

"Looks like I'm vaccinating pets as long as work is okay with it."

"Oh, and if you want to put some advertising material and signs around, it will be good exposure for your clinic."

"Leave it with me. I'll have a chat with the boss and see how we can help."

"I owe you!"

"Cocktails and ice-cream after the big day?"

"Done."

"I'll let you know by the end of the week at the latest."

"See you tomorrow."

Belle grabbed her sandwich from the fridge and ate lunch at her desk while reviewing her checklist. The Pet Expo was progressing well.

During the afternoon, Belle immersed herself in double checking all the outstanding documents. The Information Packs which would be available for all attendees still needed to be printed and collated. The Rules for Dog Registration, the Location of Council Dog Parks and the Sponsor's Advertising Brochures were all ready for printing but the Guide for New Pet Owners and How to Combat Barking Dogs were still with Frank and Kevin for updating.

Frank had said his would be ready by Wednesday so all Belle could really do was wait until then and hope for the best. If they weren't ready, she'd allowed a couple of extra days as the pack could wait until next week if necessary. That would give her some time to complete the updates herself.

By the end of the day, when everyone else had gone home, and Belle was sitting alone at her desk, only one group of emails had yet to be actioned. The sponsors. She probably should have tackled this group first but they needed time and effort which would now be available since everything else was in motion. She'll start it first thing tomorrow.

At 6.30pm as Belle turned off her computer and picked up her handbag, she wondered how Lucy had managed Paige and if anything else had happened during the day. Lucy's latest text was very uninformative, it was all about Noah and how they were having pizza at home tonight, Belle hoped they'd saved her a piece.

chapter twenty-four

Earlier that day, it was lunchtime before Lucy and Paige returned to the office after speaking to Sgt Harris. Lucy turned to Paige and asked, "Let's go to the Plaza and have a break from this place. We could both use it."

"Okay," answered Paige quietly, "I'll meet you downstairs."

Paige picked up her handbag and headed to the Ladies while Lucy checked that Kelly was happy to continue watching the front desk.

As they walk the short distance to the Plaza shopping centre, both women were lost in their own thoughts. They naturally gravitated to the coffee shop which was favoured by their team. The baguettes and paninis were wonderful and it had the best coffee in the centre. After ordering, Lucy looked at Paige with sad eyes and said "Paige, you have to tell me what's going on."

"What do you mean?"

"Something is up," Lucy said, "You're lying to the police and to us. You said you were in the office all morning and then had lunch at your desk before covering for me at the front desk."

"Yeah, that's right," stammered Paige, "You saw me."

"No, it's not right," Lucy replied, "I saw you at 1.00pm but not before that. And you asked me if I'd met Noah for lunch because you saw his van in the carpark, but how could you see this unless you were in the carpark and not in the office?"

"Umm …"

"And Frank said he saw you in the carpark talking to some bloke through his car window when he left for lunch at about 11.30am. Who was it?"

Paige looked like a deer stuck in headlights, "I didn't realise Frank saw me. I noticed him getting into his car but didn't think he'd seen me."

"Well, he did. Who were you meeting? And how long were you there?"

"I was out of the office for less than ten minutes," Paige exclaimed, "And if I was in the carpark I couldn't have been killing Jane."

"There's still over an hour unaccounted for. And why didn't you tell the police that you left the office? And why did you lie to us?"

Lucy watched Paige as she tried to think of a way out of this and saw the dejected expression when Paige realised there was no way out.

"I had a party to go to on Tuesday night and thought I'd like to liven things up a bit."

"You went to a party on a week night?" Lucy suddenly felt very old.

"Not a big one, just a few mates getting together," replied Paige, "And I have another friend who can get various … things to help with the fun."

Lucy looked directly at Paige, "Right."

"That was the friend I met in the carpark. He was dropping off the stuff."

"Why didn't you just say that you popped out to meet a friend then?"

"What if anyone asked why I was meeting him? What would I say then? The police would want to know who my friend was and I didn't want to make any trouble for him."

"What time did you meet him? What's his name?"

"It was about 11.35am because I left as soon as you went to collect the mail."

"And his name?"

"Chris."

"How long were you with Chris?"

"No more than ten minutes, I swear."

"And then where did you go?"

"Just like I said, I went back upstairs, got my lunch and ate at my desk until I relieved you."

"And nobody saw you?"

"I don't know. I didn't talk to anyone, I was on my phone then working. My desk is in the corner, I guess no-one noticed me."

Lucy considered her options. Paige had confessed to being out in the carpark but was adamant that was the only blip in her story. Why then was she reacting so strangely to the police and what about her unusual

Instagram posts? Should she push Paige more and see what came out or be happy with the information she had? Bugger it, Lucy needed to know.

"Okay, you didn't want the police questioning you about your alibi so you lied to them but your reaction this morning was extreme. You looked petrified when we passed in the corridor and when I asked you to come to the conference room, you nearly fainted. Are you really that scared about the 'party things'?"

"I'm scared they'll think I killed Jane," admitted Paige.

"Why should they think that? Did you?"

"No. I keep telling you that. But I've said some pretty mean things about her. And there have been days when I would have like to smack her."

"Everyone in the office has said things about her and I'm pretty sure most of us have wanted to slap her at some point. Is that all? You lied to the police about your alibi and are worried because you were nasty towards her?"

Paige nodded.

"So why all the strange posts on Instagram? 'If you tell the truth, you don't have to remember anything.' and 'The truth is rarely pure and never simple.' Why have you started putting up these quotes about truth?" asked Lucy.

"I feel bad about lying to the police and this is just a reminder to myself that this drama won't go on forever. I like motivational sayings and thought it might make me feel better."

"It's not going to get any better until the murderer is found and if the police spend all their time investigating you, because you lied to them, then the real murderer won't be caught." Lucy's anger was beginning to show, "You need to tell the police the truth and hopefully they'll find another suspect, the right one."

"You believe me?" asked Paige, "Do you think the police will believe me?"

Lucy stared at Paige in disbelief. How self-centred could she be? A woman had died, admittedly a nasty woman, the police were scrambling to find the killer, Lucy had been unfairly identified as the main suspect and all Paige could do was lie and think about how she herself was impacted. All this drama because Paige was so overwhelmed by her own nearly insignificant actions and because she had no regard to how they affected anyone around her.

Lunch interrupted the conversation and after some desultory chatter, they were soon headed back to the office, neither really happy with the outcome. No more was said about the murder and they went about their own jobs successfully avoiding each other for the rest of the day. The afternoon passed quickly, especially for Lucy who returned to find a message from Noah proposing dinner.

No longer the main suspect and a gorgeous dinner date; what more could Lucy ask for?

chapter twenty-five

Lucy left work immediately the clock showed 5.00pm and hurried home to change and clean up. Noah was bringing the beer and they'd order a delivery pizza but Lucy wanted to make sure her home was relatively tidy.

Belle walked in their front door just as Lucy and Noah were finishing dinner. They were sitting on the floor, near the coffee table which contained two empty beer bottles and two plates with pizza crusts as evidence of a meal for two having been eaten.

"Hi," said Belle kicking off her shoes as she came inside, "I hope you saved a piece of pizza for me."

"Of course we did," replied Lucy, "It's in the fridge."

Belle went to the kitchen, heated her late dinner and returned to the loungeroom.

"Good news," Lucy starts, "I'm no longer the main suspect."

"That is good news. How did that come about?"

Lucy explained her conversation with Sgt Harris this morning and how Rachel Donner had confirmed Lucy's alibi, "I can't believe I forgot helping Rachel with her boxes to her car. I suppose I had other things on my mind."

"Did you see anything when helping with the boxes?" asked Noah.

Lucy blushed, "I wasn't really looking. I was trying to get back to the office in case you asked me to lunch."

Noah smiled and started to reply.

"And what did Paige have to say for herself?" Belle interrupted, bringing the conversation back to the murder.

"Sgt Harris seems to have shifted his focus from me to Paige," said Lucy, "And it won't help that she's been lying to them from the beginning."

"We worked that out," Belle quipped, "Did you find out the truth?"

"Yeah and its mainly Paige being a drama queen," Lucy went on to explain about Chris, the 'party favours' and Paige's paranoia that the police will think she killed Jane because she said a few mean things about her.

"Do you think that Paige killed her?" asked Belle, "And do the police think she is guilty? The motive she's given them is similar to yours."

"I think Paige needs to be careful. She's adamant about not telling the police about Chris in case they want more information but I told her she was making a big mistake," mused Lucy, "Anyway, how was your day?"

"I finally think I have the Pet Expo under control. The winners and losers for both competitions have been notified. I've asked the successful cooks to send in their ingredient requirements and I've confirmed with all the exhibitors."

"We had one hiccup," Belle continued, "One of the vets pulled out due to a scheduling conflict. But I rang Georgie and she's checking if one of her vets will help."

Belle was on a roll, "Tomorrow I'm going to contact the Sponsors to finalise their requirements and that will leave the immediate jobs of getting Arthur to complete the Placement Map plus Frank and Kevin to finish updating the guides."

"You've done well."

"Thanks. If I can finally get the Placement Map from Arthur, I can let the cooks, tasters, exhibitors and sponsors where they need to be on the day. I also thought it would be a good opportunity to have another chat with Arthur now we know his alibi. He might let something else slip."

"Good idea. If he was out in the carpark on his way to church, he might have seen something," replied Lucy, "Do we know why the police are so interested in people who were out of the office at the time? It seems strange."

"No but the only link Jules could see between the people who were reinterviewed was that they'd left the office for lunch."

Noah had been sitting quietly while the twins pondered these developments.

"Why are you looking into the death?" he asked.

"The police were concentrating on Lucy to the exclusion of anybody else, so we had to investigate," Belle exclaimed, "My sister wasn't going to jail for a crime she didn't commit."

"Does that mean you're going to stop now that Lucy isn't the main suspect anymore?"

The twins looked at each other, this was something they hadn't considered in their search for the truth.

"I suppose we could leave it to the police?" queried Lucy.

"I guess so. But we've found out things the police haven't and honestly, I've quite enjoyed it. Except for the part where you might go to jail."

Noah looked confused, "I thought you would have been happy with Jane's death. She was a horrible bully and the world is a nicer place without her; everyone's said so."

"Jane was not a nice woman but she was part of our team. Not everyone thinks this was a good thing. Even Frank said today that the office was missing something since she's not there."

"But she was so mean to everyone and I've heard all of you complaining about her nosiness? Why do you care how she died?" questioned Noah.

Belle stared at Noah, "You're right. I didn't like her. She was horrible to me and everyone else in the office. She was opinionated and expressed those opinions whether you wanted to hear them or not; she was lazy and the office is certainly a better place to be since she's not there, she was a terrible gossip and hurt many people with her comments …"

"So, why is finding out what happened so important to you?"

"None of that excuses murder. No-one had the right to end her life. She had dreams; she had plans; Las Vegas doesn't appeal to me but she wanted to go and experience it. As ghastly as she was, no-one was entitled to kill her."

"So, you think that people can be as awful as they want, treat others with such disrespect and we have to accept it?" Noah's annoyance was starting to show.

"No, we don't have to accept it," Belle replied, "But there are a lot of options between putting up with bad behaviour and killing someone."

"Nobody here seemed to be doing anything to improve her behaviour, even last week Lucy was complaining about how nasty she was."

"You're siding with the killer?" exclaimed Belle.

Noah back tracked quickly, "No, of course not. But I don't understand why you feel so strongly about someone who you criticised so much a short while ago."

"How do you know what I said about Jane?" asked Belle.

Lucy blushed, "Noah and I may have discussed the murder over dinner on Friday night. He was interested in what was happening and I might have exaggerated how everyone in the office hated her."

"She wasn't liked by people in the office but I think some people are surprised by how much they are missing her presence," mused Belle, "It's strange how people react to change, even if the change is good."

"So, you agree that her death was a good thing, a good change?" said Noah.

"No. I'm glad I don't have to deal with her any more but murder, any murder, is wrong," Belle stated bluntly, "Anyway, I'm going to bed. Good night."

Belle called to Cooper and after a quick pitstop outside, they went off to bed, leaving Lucy and Noah staring after them.

"I'm sorry if I upset her," Noah apologised, "I didn't mean anything by it."

"It's fine," Lucy replied, "She's had a long day and is probably overtired. She gets like that sometimes."

"Umm. As long as you're not putting yourself in any danger," Noah continued, "I wouldn't want you to get hurt."

"You're sweet. I doubt I'm in any danger but I will be careful if it makes you happy."

And with that, the evening ended on a nice note.

chapter twenty-six

Tuesday in the office seemed brighter. It was as if the team was becoming accustomed to Jane not being there. Between the distance of time, helped by the weekend, and a release of tension regarding the Pet Expo through Belle's status update yesterday, there was a noticeable lightening of spirits.

There was chatter in the kitchen as different people brewed their morning coffees and Kelly was even heard to be laughing at one of Frank's corny jokes.

The only exception was Paige. Her distress was quite plain for anyone to see. The changing of 'chief police suspect' from Lucy to Paige was having a dramatic effect. Both Lucy and Belle approached Paige separately during the morning only to be firmly rebuffed. It seemed like Paige wanted to work it out for herself.

Belle spent the morning contacting the Pet Expo sponsors, making sure they were happy with the placement of their logos in the advertising materials, noting any special requirements for the day and agreeing on delivery dates for other sponsor marketing materials such as bunting for the event, monogrammed prizes for entrants and those all-important food bowls for the doggie taste testers to use during the competition.

Just before lunch, Belle approached Arthur, with some trepidation. Was today's Arthur going to be the remorseful man from last week, or had his long weekend turned him back to normal? She really wasn't in the mood for a fight but she'd also had enough of Arthur's nonsense. And she needed to see if he knew anything else about Jane's murder.

"Arthur, have you finished the Placement Map?" Belle asked as she walked towards his desk.

"You know I was away yesterday," Arthur replied, not looking away from his computer screen.

"Yes, but it was supposed to be finished last week."

"It's been busy in the office if you haven't noticed," Arthur dismissed Belle, "I'll get to it soon."

"No," Belle raised her voice to get Arthur's attention, "The Placement Map is critical and we only have just over two weeks before the expo so you will finish it urgently and have a copy to me by tomorrow night."

"Since when are you in charge?"

"Since the date for Pet Expo is getting close and things need to be done," Belle snapped back as she turned to leave, "And you need to do your part."

"Oh, and when did you last see Jane? And when did you last go into the photocopier room? What did you see in the car park?" Belle peppered him with questions, forgetting to be subtle and hoping in a vague way that he might answer something, "There must have been a reason why the police wanted to interview you again. And why are they interested in people who left the building?"

"I told the police, I told Jack, and I'm telling you for the last time; I didn't kill her."

Arthur's face was a shade of bright cherry red and his hands were clenched into tight fists by his side as he stood behind his desk.

"I suppose I last saw Jane around morning tea time, or it may have been later. It was a quiet day, nothing was really happening so nothing stands out. I went to my church and met with my priest during my lunch break and by the time I got back at 1.00pm, the 'Out of Order' sign was up on the photocopier room so I guess the last time I was in there was before lunch," Arthur took a deep breath, "I can't remember anything unusual in the carpark, there were the normal tradies, the normal delivery people, I suppose the only difference was that group of school children getting onto a school bus."

"Why didn't you mention them before?" asked Belle.

"I didn't think about it and do you really think a group of kids had anything to do with it?"

"No, not really," Belle was downcast, "I guess you didn't know anything."

"Humpf." Arthur turned away.

"Hold on," Belle said, "Did you say the 'Out of Order' sign was on the door at 1.00pm?"

"Yes. When I got back from lunch, I wanted to collect some printing but the door was shut with the sign up. I looked for Lucy to complain, but she was at lunch so I had to wait until she got back and you know the rest."

Belle smiled to herself, "Yes we all know what happened next. Don't forget, the Placement Map to me by tomorrow night."

****

Charlie was the last friend to arrive at dinner this Tuesday night.

"There are lots of rumblings at work about your murder," she announced.

Lucy immediately turned her attention to Charlie, "What happened?"

"Nothing, and that's the problem. I heard Harris complaining that every lead was circumstantial and seemed to go nowhere," Charlie continued, "But at least you're in the clear now so all this investigating can stop and the police can be left to do their job."

There were some murmurings around the table.

"I don't want to give up," replied Belle, "I've sort of liked the investigating. It's like solving a complicated puzzle and you know how I love puzzles."

Charlie shook her head while Lucy wavered, "On one hand I feel really sorry for Paige, she was taking it so hard today and I don't actually think she did it. On the other hand, she is so selfish, maybe some time as the chief suspect will teach her a lesson."

Jules interrupted, "I think we should continue. We've been making some progress and I feel some sense of responsibility for Paige working in your office. I was involved in her getting the job."

Belle asked, "Georgie, what do you think?'

"Now that Lucy is no longer suspected, I don't feel the same pressure to investigate but I'm happy to keep going if everyone else wants to."

"Charlie?"

"You already know my feelings about this."

"We really haven't looked at Mark or Jack closely yet. How about we see if there's anything unusual and decide after that?

There was a general nodding of heads at Belle's suggestion.

"And I still want to see what Kevin is up to with all these online auctions," added Georgie.

"And have you got Jane's laptop here?" Jules asked, "I can search her hard drive for any clues."

Lucy passed Jane's laptop and the external hard drives to Jules, pointing out the sticker with the password stuck to the screen inside.

"Do we toss for Mark and Jack?" Lucy joked.

"No, I want Jack" Belle replied.

"Do you now?" Georgie teased.

Belle blushed, "I need to talk to Jack about the Pet Expo and I thought if I had lunch with him away from the office, it would be a chance to ask him about Jane and her gambling on the horses too."

"Sure," Georgie did not look convinced.

"Any suggestions for how I tackle Mark then?" Lucy pondered.

"You could take him out for lunch?" Georgie suggested with a sly look towards Belle.

"Shut up," Belle looked directly at Georgie, "Do you have any excuse you could use to see him in his office?"

"What's happening with Jane's work? I bet you're doing it without saying anything." Jules asked, "Maybe you could ask to see him to discuss your workload and Jane's job and that should give you an easy excuse to talk about Jane's gambling and her shares."

"That could work," Lucy agreed, "But how do I ask him about cheating the tax department? It's not something that I can just blurt out."

There was quiet around the table as this question was considered. Charlie looked at them all and said, "How can you think you are investigators if this stumps you?"

"What would you do?"

"Easy. Start the conversation with Jane's shares, talk about what happens to them now and how the tax department is bound to take a large proportion of the proceeds and if he doesn't offer his solution, you can ask if he knows of any ways to avoid paying large amounts of tax."

"That's good," Lucy was impressed, "Thanks guys. Sounds like we have a plan."

"And something else I found out today," Belle said, "In all his rantings this morning, Arthur let slip that the 'Out of Order' sign was hanging from the photocopier room door at 1.00pm when he returned from lunch. Assuming the killer placed the sign on the door as they left, that reduces our timeframe by an hour or so."

"That's a good bit of information," Jules said enthusiastically, "I'll add it to the spreadsheet tonight and see if anything changes with our suspects."

Belle hid a slight smile; it seems everyone was having as much fun as her with this investigating lark. Except Charlie. Charlie did not look happy as the rest of the table decided on their menu choices while chattering about the investigation.

chapter twenty-seven

The following morning the twins took diametrically opposite approaches to their next tasks.

Belle decided to dive right in and ask Jack for a lunch meeting immediately. As soon as she saw Jack, she said those dreaded words, 'we need to talk' and with some trepidation, Jack agreed to have lunch together in the courtyard and discuss the status of the Pet Expo.

Lucy on the other hand, floated from one job to the next for most of the morning, hoping an opportunity to talk to Mark would just appear.

As was often the case, things tend to work out for those who don't plan. Just before lunch, Mark walked up to Lucy and asked her about the progress of one of Jane's jobs.

"Why should I know the latest monthly statistics for how many residents have complained about their neighbours' pets? That was Jane's job, not mine."

"Sorry, I thought you were looking after it," replied Mark with no contrition.

"Mark, could we please talk about what is going to happen with Jane's job?" asked Lucy.

"Of course. I've discussed it ..."

"Mark, could we go to your office and talk about this in private please?"

Mark looked very uncomfortable, "That's probably a good idea. Is now a suitable time?"

Lucy nodded and they left the general office after asking Paige to keep an eye on the reception desk.

Mark arranged himself behind his desk while Lucy sat in a chair opposite.

"I was going to speak to you later," Mark began, "When things were a bit more settled. I've been speaking with the Mayor and we've decided not to replace Jane at this time."

"But ..."

"We've decided it's a waste of resources to have a receptionist position when more and more people are completing their tasks online and our face to face customers have significantly dropped this financial year."

"So, I'm out of a job? Just like that?" Lucy questioned.

"No. As I was saying, it is quite fortuitous that Jane is no longer working for the council. The mayor has agreed to move you to Jane's position as an Assistant Animal Control Officer in the short term which will leave the receptionist position vacant and help us with balancing the budget."

"It's not fortuitous, it's murder," Lucy was appalled by Mark's lack of empathy, "What's going to happen to the reception area?"

Lucy thought about all the time she'd spent making it a welcoming space for council residents. Was that time all wasted now?

"The screen will stay down from next Monday with a sign directing people to use the phone to call the number which is applicable to their enquiry. There will also be a list of numbers for our team members and for specific roles."

"And who is going to be doing everything else I did?"

"I thought you and I could sit down at the end of next week once you've had some time to think about it and divide up the tasks between the rest of the team. What do you think?"

"You said I would be moved to Animal Control in the short term, what will happen after that?"

"Jane's job will be advertised. You can obviously apply for it and with your experience you have a good chance of getting it," Mark was quite circumspect about Lucy's future with no comprehension of how his words were bringing her world crashing down.

"What if I don't want Jane's job? Or what if I don't get Jane's job? Do I get any say in this?"

Mark finally began to show some inkling of the havoc he was creating, "I'm sorry, the restructure is going to happen. But you do have options. If you really don't want to move into Animal Control, you can elect to be placed on the redeployee pool. Then you will possibly be redeployed elsewhere within the council. However, it is a gamble, there is no guarantee that you'll be able to choose where you end up or if you will even like it."

Lucy was near to tears and looked away. Here was Mark tearing her work world apart and giving her the perfect opening to ask about Jane's gambling at the same time. Surely Belle and the rest would understand if she concentrated on her own job now. No, she had agreed to ask Mark about share trading and she didn't want to let her friends down. Her own job would work out and if it didn't, she could always find another. Maybe it was time to branch out on her own and try something new. That decided, Lucy turned back to Mark, "Talking about gambling …"

Mark started squirming in his chair.

"When we went to Jane's house to find the permits, we found all this paperwork about share trading. Did you know Jane was buying and selling shares?" Lucy asked.

"She may have mentioned it," admitted Mark, "Why do you ask?"

"You do lots of share trading and I thought you guys might have compared notes and discussed what you were buying and selling?"

"I did a lot of talking that's for sure," Mark grumbled.

"What do you mean?"

"Nothing."

"No, what did you mean by saying that you did the talking?"

"I suppose it doesn't matter now but Jane was being a pain."

Mark went on to explain that Jane had overheard him discussing some shares with one of his contacts who happened to be a supplier for the council's maintenance section. Even though there was nothing shady about the deal, it could be argued that there was a conflict of interest. Someone could say that the supplier had gotten the council contract as a result of providing stock trading information to Mark.

When Jane put it all together, she approached Mark and asked him to pass the information from his contact to her too.

"She spoke about how the previous Mayor had to leave because of suspicious deals and how the new Mayor was so by the book," Mark grimaced, "She didn't threaten me outright but certainly made it clear what would happen if I didn't pass on the information."

Lucy stared at Mark. Didn't he realise that he'd just given himself a serious motive for killing Jane?

"Did you pass on the information?"

Mark nodded.

"Did Jane make lots of money from it?"

Mark nodded again.

"How long has this been going on?" Lucy asked.

"Not long."

"But if both of you have been making all this money from share trading, doesn't it affect your tax?" Lucy queried, watching carefully for Mark's reaction.

Mark started laughing, "She was such a nosy person. Yes, all that extra income could affect how much tax you have to pay but I've got a system."

Mark launched into a myriad of details about tax, shares, timings, and bank loans until Lucy's head was spinning.

"But how could your system help Jane avoid tax?"

"I told you, she was a nosy old bat. I posted my tax avoidance system on Facebook last month for one of my contacts, not really thinking that anyone else would be paying attention and she saw it. I didn't even know she was following me."

"And ..."

"And she made me explain it in detail so she could use it too."

Mark started shifting papers around, signalling the end of the conversation.

"Why did you tell me all of this?" Lucy asked, "Aren't you worried that I'll want the same thing as Jane?"

"No. You're too honest," Mark replied, "My only fear is that you'll tell the police but then it's only your word against mine. And I didn't kill her, so they won't be able to find anything that says I did."

Lucy got up from her chair and turned to leave when Mark said, "About Jane's job, keep it to yourself for now. If anyone asks, just say that nothing's been decided yet and everyone needs to chip in."

"Okay, but I'm not lying to Belle if she asks."

Mark nodded in resignation, "No-one else."

As Lucy left Mark's office, she wondered if the murderer would further regret their actions when their own workload increased.

chapter twenty-eight

As Belle and Jack walked past Mark's office, the door was tightly shut. Belle assumed that Lucy was in there with Mark and hopefully getting all the information that they needed. Now if only she managed the same thing with Jack.

Belle had spent the morning composing a list of questions for Jack, both about the expo and betting on the horses. It was surprising how many questions she had about horse racing; Belle was not a gambler in the true sense, generally only betting on the Melbourne Cup once a year. But she'd had a flutter on The Everest this year, everyone had been talking about the new horse race in Sydney worth millions of dollars and her lucky $10.00 wager had nearly doubled.

Jack had led the way to a sunny bench on the far side of the courtyard. Even if anyone saw them, it was unlikely they'd be disturbed. They both opened their lunches and, as they ate their sandwiches, Belle spoke about the expo. She gave Jack an update on the current status of the exhibitors, the suppliers, the competition winners and losers and then spoke about the guides being updated by Kevin and Frank. Jack was impressed by Belle's work and said as much.

"Wait until I finish before thanking me," Belle joked, "I may have a problem with Arthur."

"May have a problem?"

"Arthur's been procrastinating with the Placement Map and as you know it's critical. I told him that it must be completed and with me by tonight but I might need you to step in if he doesn't produce it on time," Belle answered Jack's question then continued, "I don't know why you gave him such an important task."

Jack was disconcerted, "I know you're mad with me about that. But I did have a reason."

"Why would you give the most important job, the job that ties everything together, the job that is the central to the whole expo, to Arthur? Haven't I shown that I deserve it?"

"Absolutely. And that's why I gave it to Arthur. He's been blatantly taking credit for all the great work you've done but he's been able to justify it so I needed something specific to catch him in a lie."

Belle was dumbfounded. Who knew Jack was so sneaky? "But what was your plan when Arthur failed to produce the map on time? The whole Pet Expo could fall in a heap."

"I knew you would keep track of it, regardless of who I assigned the task to," Jack was casual in his dismissal of the potential landmine, "Now I know the deadline, I'll check with Arthur tomorrow and follow up if he hasn't finished it."

"I can't believe you gambled on the success of the Pet Expo."

"Wasn't much of a gamble. I've certainly risked more in the past."

"Yeah I heard you liked going to the races but I didn't realise you actually gambled and risked something?"

"Gambling is always a risk, you can obviously lose your stake but you can also quickly get in over your head before you realise it," Jack replied, "A couple of my friends have sailed dangerously close to losing everything. And there was even a time when gambling was taking over my life. So, yes, gambling is risky."

"I didn't know."

"No reason why you should. I rarely talk about it at work."

"Did you talk with Jane about it?" Belle asked, "While we were looking for the Pet Expo permits we came across all these papers about betting on the horse racing. She seems to have been gambling for quite a long time."

"No or at least we only spoke about it in passing," Jack replied, "A couple of weeks ago, she overheard me telling Frank that I was going to the races on the following day and she asked me what horses I was going to back. I remember because she was really strange about it. Everyone is always asking everyone else who they fancy so it was nothing new for me but Jane seemed to take it very seriously. Anyway, none of my selections did any good and she never asked me for any tips after that."

Jack chuckled and Belle smiled. From Jane's records, there was plenty of evidence that she only liked to back certainties, if there was such a thing in racing. Maybe that was why she only dabbled in scratchies and horses and put her serious attention to the stock market?

Belle thought back to all the questions she had about horseracing and why Jane would think she could win and decided to just ask Jack for his opinion, "Jack why would anyone think that they could win money betting on horses?"

"Some people do I guess. But it's normally the really rich people who can place gigantic, complicated bets that do end up winning. There's a saying that people in the horseracing industry generally pay for their hobby, and it's only the lucky few that actually make a decent profit."

"What draws you to it then if it's not the winning?" Belle asked.

"Actually, it's not just me. There's a bunch of blokes from school who go to the races every now and then. Us single fellas go more regularly but our married friends try and make it sometimes too. It's a good way to keep in touch with friends over a few beers and bets."

"I get that. There's a group of us from school who catch up for dinner each week for the same reason."

"And I love looking at the horses. They are majestic animals with such great individual personalities. Some days I envy the jockeys and trainers for the close relationships they have with these wonderful creatures."

"Have you ever thought about joining the horseracing industry in some way?"

"No, it's not for me. I have other plans for my life."

Belle wondered whether Jack would talk about his political aspirations. After Georgie had mentioned Jack's Facebook page, Belle had logged in and had a sly look and it seemed that Jack was indeed planning to run for office at some point in his career.

Jack looked at Belle's interested face, "It's not something I talk about but one day I would like to be involved in politics."

"And you think politics and horseracing don't mesh well?" Belle quipped.

Jack laughed, "I think they go together very well. Bob Hawke was one of our most popular Prime Ministers and he was known for liking a punt."

"Aiming high then?"

"Maybe."

Belle smiled, their lunch break was nearly over and it was time to return the conversation to the expo, "Along those lines, another thing I need you to do is to confirm with the Mayor that he is willing and available to open the Expo."

"I can do that. Is there anything else I can help with?"

"We're going to need some extra Council staff to help with the set up, then during the expo and finally cleaning everything up afterwards. I was hoping you could speak with your counterparts and arrange for some volunteers?"

"Do you have a specific number of people in mind?"

"No, it really depends on how many volunteers we get as to how we can utilise them."

"All right, I'll put the word out and see what sort of numbers we get."

"Thanks for that and thanks for having lunch with me, it was good to go through everything with you. Now we wait and see if Arthur meets his deadline," Belle joked.

"Anytime. I like having lunch with you," replied Jack.

Belle felt her spirits rise for the first time in many days. She may not have found out anything useful and only sort of clarified a few questions but this had been a lovely lunch. It was probably lucky she hadn't had her revenge on Arthur and Jack yet. Maybe this investigation will produce more than just finding the murderer. Providing Jack was telling the truth. Belle hoped he was.

chapter twenty-nine

Lucy spent most of the rest of the day staring into space, thinking about her options. Should she stay or should she go? Should she try the redeployee pool and see what happened? What was that saying? 'Better the devil you know!' Maybe telling Belle would help.

"Lucy?" said a voice in the distance, "Lucy!"

Lucy looked up from her musings to see Belle standing next to her desk. Another 'devil' saying sprang to mind, 'Speak of the devil and it appears.' She wasn't sure that Belle would like to be compared to the devil but it seemed appropriate in the moment.

"What?"

"Are you okay? I've been standing her for nearly ten minutes," Belle replied.

"No, you haven't. Stop exaggerating," Lucy grumbled.

"It felt like it," Belle replied, "Did you get the information from Mark?"

"More than I wanted," Lucy mumbled.

"What did he say?"

"I'll tell you later."

Belle looked confused. Lucy was acting strangely. What had Mark said? Did he confess? And to what; murder, fraud, insider trading, tax evasion? Was Lucy deciding what to tell the police?

"If that's what you want. I asked Jules over for dinner so we could add all the latest information to the spreadsheet but she and Drew are eating with his mother and discussing wedding venues. Apparently they're still arguing over having it at the church. Jules is going to email the latest version of the spreadsheet but it's just us for dinner."

"Okay."

"Do you want me to pick up something on the way home? Or would you prefer to order in?"

"Whatever you want."

Belle was starting to get concerned. It was unheard of for Lucy not to have an opinion on their food.

"Are you sure everything is okay?"

"Later," Lucy gave Belle a slight smile.

Belle nodded, "See you at home and I'll stop at the shops on the way there."

By the time Belle got home with dinner, Lucy was curled up on the couch with Cooper and a large glass of wine.

"Does that wine go with chocolate ice-cream?" she asked Lucy, pulling some from a shopping bag.

"Everything goes with chocolate ice-cream," Lucy smiled reaching for the container, "Can you get me a spoon?"

Belle brought over a spoon and sat on the end of the couch, shoving Cooper off, "What happened?"

"Mark told me that my job is going."

"What?"

"It's not as bad as it sounds. He offered me Jane's job in the short term or I can go on the redeployee list. But I'm thinking it might be time to do something different."

"What would you do?"

"I have no idea. I thought I'd take Jane's job for now and seriously start looking at what I'd like to do. I might even go back and study."

"I think that's a good idea. You could even take some time off and travel."

"You just want to have this place to yourself," Lucy joked.

The twins discussed the different options open for Lucy while they finished the ice-cream and then moved on to salted cashew nuts and chocolate biscuits. Belle knew what comfort food to buy when Lucy was down and had come home well stocked.

Lucy licked salt from her fingers, having finished the last of the cashews, "Aren't you going to ask me what else he said?"

"Did you find out something? I didn't want to ask."

"The main thing that stood out is Mark is not a nice person," Lucy started, "He said Jane was being a 'pain' and called her murder 'fortuitous' because it's going to help him manage the department's budget and he didn't care about the havoc he was creating for me."

"Nothing new there."

"But you should have seen him when I mentioned gambling."

Lucy went on to explain how uncomfortable Mark became with the conversation and then let slip about Jane effectively blackmailing him. She described the setup with the potential conflict of interest and reminded Belle about the Mayor's feelings concerning scandals.

"And he copped to the tax system as well. Although I didn't understand how it worked, he was quite happy to explain it to me and say that Jane was using it."

"Do you think he did it?"

"I don't know. He certainly had a good motive with basically being blackmailed but when I asked why he was happy to tell me everything, he said that the police wouldn't find anything against him because he didn't do it. And he didn't sound guilty, more disgruntled really."

"Umm."

"On the other hand, this murderer had no thought for how this would impact on the office and all the extra work we would have to do and that reeks of Mark and his absolute lack of empathy for anyone else."

Belle looked at Lucy, "I doubt the murderer considered our workloads while bashing Jane's head in."

"I suppose but you can't deny that Mark makes a good suspect and his contact too. They might have thought that Jane was a loose cannon and had to go to protect them and teamed up to do it."

"It's certainly possible, if we can just work out how an outsider got into the photocopier room. And it's good you think they're possible suspects because I don't think Jack was involved."

"Why? What did he say?"

"Nothing earth shattering, we spoke about horse racing and gambling but little to do with Jane. And we talked about the Pet Expo and Arthur."

Belle explained Jack's reasoning about Arthur and catching him in a definite lie.

"That's good news at least. Better than him just ignoring it like you thought he was doing."

"But it was a big gamble. What if I didn't keep track of everything as he expected?"

Lucy laughed and shook her head.

"Okay it wasn't a big risk," Belle said, "I just hope Jack was telling the truth."

Lucy heard Belle's wistful tone and wondered, not for the first time, if her twin was headed for an office romance. Which brought Noah to mind. Maybe they could have dinner this weekend? She'd missed Noah during his regular Tuesday delivery yesterday so hadn't seen him since that unusual conversation on Monday night. The sooner the police found this murderer, the sooner they could all get back to normal.

chapter thirty

B elle picked up the empty ice-cream container and took it to the kitchen, "Let's get a pizza and we can add all this information to the spreadsheet. Jules said she would send the latest copy, can you check your email."

Lucy opened up her laptop, "Yeah it's here and there's a long note from Jules too."

Lucy read the email while Belle ordered the pizza. She became engrossed in the note, then opened several attachments and was eagerly reading them when Belle returned.

"It's looking serious for Mark," Lucy had become quite sombre. Belle sat down and started reading.

Jules's email told the twins of her efforts with Jane's computer. She detailed the four files devoted to Jane's different gambling habits. The Las Vegas spreadsheet revealed no further information but tucked in between the financial year sheets from the Shares spreadsheet was a hidden sheet titled Tips.

Here Jane had listed every tip she had been provided, when she received the information and if she benefited from the tip. In earlier times, Mark had merely featured amongst several names but towards the end, he was the only tipster and as the benefits increased, the tips were becoming more frequent. In addition to the rising rate of the tips, it had been going on much longer that Mark had admitted. He'd lied. And if he'd lied about this, what else had he lied about?

The Scratchies spreadsheet provided little detail, Jane obviously liked the tickets for the fun of them without actually expecting any financial gain and this was apparent from both the lack of detail she kept and the infrequency of her purchases. It was more of a wish than a plan.

On the other hand, the Horse Racing spreadsheet was very detailed. The dates indicated that this was a newer venture but no lesser an obsession than the share trading. She also had a Horse Racing sheet called Tips but unlike the Shares sheet it wasn't hidden. There were only a couple of names with Jack being one of the first. It showed clearly that Jack's tips were not profitable hence the reason why he only appeared that once. It seemed that Jack had been telling the truth.

Lucy opened the murder spreadsheet and started entering the new information; Mark's stronger motive with Jane blackmailing him and her demands coming more frequently; Paige's actual alibi; and Jack's lack of motive now the horseracing tips had been explained.

"Did Jules add the bit about the 'Out of Order' sign being up at 1.00pm?"

"Yes, it's here."

"If the sign was up at 1.00pm, then it's probable that the murder happened before that so let's look at who had lunch at what time to see who was around."

Lucy started highlighting different entries in the spreadsheet, "Mark, Paige, Frank and Arthur all had lunch between 12.00pm and 1.00pm. Jack, Kelly and Kevin had lunch between 1.00pm and 2.00pm."

"I really don't think Jack or Kelly are involved with this," Belle replied, "That only leaves Kevin in the late lunches.

"I understand why you don't suspect Jack, but why do you think Kelly is in the clear?"

"She's my friend and I trust her. Of all the people in the office, she is the one person I can rely on. Excluding family of course," Belle quickly added as Lucy opened her mouth to object, "And she made a good point about killing Jane and then calmly having lunch with me. I think I would have noticed something."

"But you said you thought she was hiding something? Shouldn't you find out what first?"

"You're right, I should find out. I'll ask her tomorrow but in the meantime, I want her off the list of suspects."

"All right, I'll tag Jack and Kelly as not involved. What about Kevin?"

"Georgie was going to investigate his interest in auctions and if that impacted at all. Why don't we leave him on the list for now but concentrate on those who had an early lunch until we hear from Georgie?"

"Sounds good," Lucy replied, "So we're down to Mark, Paige, Frank and Arthur. And strangely, they were the people the police reinterviewed. Maybe it wasn't to do with those who left the building for lunch but more to do with what time they had lunch? Perhaps Arthur blurted about the sign when the police originally interviewed him and they have been focussed on an earlier murder all along?"

"Let's look at what we have on each of them."

After flicking between different sheets, it seemed they had amassed a variety of information on all four suspects in the last week.

Lucy expressed sympathy for Paige. The evidence against Paige was just as circumstantial as it had been for Lucy. The major difference was that Paige had lied and was continuing to make some questionable choices. Except for the ten minutes she claimed to be in the car park, it was possible that she had been in the office having her lunch until she relieved Lucy at the front counter at 1.00pm. Unfortunately, she had lied once and it was feasible that she was still lying, although Lucy didn't think so.

And while the motive of ruined clothes and eavesdropping seemed fanciful, Paige was only young and may have been overwhelmed by her emotions if she felt threatened and lashed out unthinkingly. Neither Belle nor Lucy believed Paige was the killer but these was still a small frisson of doubt. They considered her a probable no; someone unlikely and also someone not high on the list to be further investigated.

And while Belle was hoping for more incriminating data, Arthur had the most unlikely motive. Excluding the general 'she was annoying' motive, the only whisper about him was possible cheating or bad temper at work but this was more gossip than anything concrete. There was no mention of him in any of Jane's computer files and neither of the twins had heard of him gambling in any form. He really was the stereotypical old man with his thinking stuck many decades earlier. And his argument with Noah at the lift confirmed his alibi of leaving work to go to the church, or at least go somewhere. Lucy and Belle considered speaking to Arthur's parish priest to check if Arthur had actually gone to the church but decided to leave that as a possible later lead if nothing else worked out.

And even though they didn't know where he went, Frank also had external confirmation of his alibi. Paige inadvertently confirmed seeing Frank getting into his car and leaving after 11.30am. But perhaps Frank killed Jane before he left, although the time would have been very close. Or perhaps he returned and whacked her before going back to his desk; he definitely had strong feelings about Jane's behaviour.

And his motive was still unknown and it was likely to remain that way. Frank was open about having a secret and yet insistent that he would not have killed to keep the secret quiet. And he said the secret was old so maybe it had lost its sting or maybe the secret had become more valuable with age. It was impossible to know unless they discovered the actual secret.

While Frank's motive was elusive, Mark's motive was becoming stronger and stronger. It started as general gossip about insider trading and progressed to actual blackmail for share tips. The results of the blackmail were clear to see in Jane's spreadsheets and Mark basically confessed as much, although he was fuzzy on the details. Then there was the dodgy tax scam. Of everyone they had investigated, Mark certainly had the most compelling motive and if Jane became indiscreet, he would certainly lose his lifestyle, his job and possibly more.

His alibi, like everyone else's, was sketchy. He claimed to be with Jack leading into lunch, then going over to the Plaza to eat. There was no way to dispute the Plaza claim but perhaps Jack could verify the early part of Mark's alibi. Maybe Jack saw Mark leave his office and head towards the carpark. That would be a job for tomorrow. But the more the twins looked at the spreadsheet and the compiled information, the worse it was looking for Mark.

"But what if he did leave?" Lucy asked.

"Maybe his contact helped him. That would make more sense for me, I have a hard time seeing Mark hit Jane but I can definitely see him setting her up."

"Yeah and we don't know who his contact is. It could be someone who already has a criminal past and would do whatever it takes to protect himself."

"We need to find out who Mark's partner is," Belle replied, "Didn't he say it was a supplier for the council's maintenance section? We could check the contracts and see which ones Mark approved and that might give us a name."

"Good idea," Lucy said, "But it doesn't solve the problem of how they got into the photocopier room."

"I've been thinking about that. Didn't you say Jane used to let people in when you weren't there? Maybe Mr Contact pretended to have a tip for Jane and lured her into the photocopier room. Mark could have told him the layout of the office and suggested a time when it was likely you wouldn't be in the office. What do you think?"

"I think that sounds very probable and much better than my idea of Mark handing over his security pass. Although surely someone would have seen a stranger walking around and commented on it?"

"Maybe not. Maybe he got lucky. Maybe we're missing something. Or maybe we're just totally wrong." Belle sounded very disheartened.

chapter thirty-one

After Belle's dismal pronouncement, the pizza delivery arrived and the surge of carbs did wonders.

"Charlie raised a good point on Tuesday night. Do we keep investigating? Does the information we've found out about Jack and Mark warrant it, especially since you're no longer under suspicion?"

"I want to keep going. We've come this far and it would be nice to solve it. And I don't think the police are getting anywhere and Paige is being railroaded, same as I was," Lucy replied.

"Charlie wouldn't let Paige be railroaded, especially if we can prove she wasn't involved."

"Charlie may not have a say," Lucy reasoned, "So you do want to continue?"

"Yeah," Belle nodded her head, "Jane was horrible but unlike what Mark and Noah think, she didn't deserve to die like that regardless of how it improves Mark's budget. And I'd like to catch the culprit."

"Maybe Mark's attitude towards letting it go is more understandable if he's the murderer or one of them at least," Lucy said, "But I don't think Noah meant it the way it came out. He's not one to condone violence, he still gets uptight about his Mum being bullied. And he was definitely apologetic once you went to bed. It was just a misunderstanding."

"I suppose," Belle didn't sound convinced but ceded to her sister, "And looking at the motives, Mark still has the most to lose and we've shown how an outsider could have been involved."

"What's our plan for tomorrow then?"

"I'll try and convince Kelly to share whatever she's hiding, I'll ask Jack if he saw Mark go towards the carpark and, if the opportunity arises, I'll ask

Frank about his motive. Could you ring Georgie and check what she's found about Kevin and his auctions?"

"Sure. And that will possibly clear Kelly, Frank and Kevin. Mark could become not only our best suspect, but our only one," Lucy replied, "Do you want me to ask Kate in Maintenance about the contracts? She looks after all the Council's supply agreements once they've been signed and probably already knows who Mark's contact is."

"Good idea, hopefully Kate will be able to help," Belle mused. "But I still feel like we're missing something."

"Something or someone?"

"One of them," Belle smiled, "Or maybe both."

****

Both Belle and Lucy started the next day with a renewed sense of enthusiasm. The aim of trying to clear everyone else except Mark gave the twins a clear focus.

Belle stopped at a local coffee shop and bought Kelly's favourite caffeine hit. When she sat by Kelly's desk with her offering, Kelly's gaze was suspicious, "What have I done to deserve this?"

"It's a bribe," Belle said bluntly, "I want to know what you're hiding about Jane."

Kelly looked around the office and lowered her voice, "It's nothing. I didn't kill her."

"I know that. And I won't tell anyone if you don't want me to but I need to know what your nothing is."

"Promise?"

Belle nodded and waited.

"I had a big fight with Jane a couple of weeks ago. It was in the kitchen and she asked me if it was true that my Hayley needed a maths tutor. And when I said yes, she made a crack about how children from a single parent home often struggled at school all due to the parents breaking up the families."

"She was such a cow!" Belle responded.

"I was so mad that I ended up pushing her out of the way with my shoulder as I walked past her."

"How come I didn't hear about this?" Belle smiled, "I would love to have seen it."

"Don't joke!" Kelly protested, "I felt so bad when she stumbled against the wall. She didn't fall and wasn't hurt but I've never done anything like that before and it felt horrible. I was so worried that someone had seen it and would think I was this violent person. And then when she was killed and all of us became suspects, I thought for sure someone would accuse me, using this as a reason."

"You have nothing to worry about. No-one would think badly of you, even if they found out about it. Which they won't from me."

Kelly smiled with a touch of relief, "I'm glad you've taken me off your list of suspects then."

"That reminds me, we need to talk about your useless privacy settings on Instagram and Facebook," Belle snorted, "But another time. Finish your coffee and let's see if Arthur has completed the Placement Map, his deadline was last night and Jack was planning to follow up today."

****

Meanwhile, Lucy was on the phone with Georgie, "Did you find anything on Kevin's auction buys?"

"No, I looked deeper into his socials and there's no pattern with either his purchases or the items he expresses interest in. I think it's like Belle said, a harmless hobby. But I wonder where his hobby comes from. It's not a common pastime these days."

"No, I suppose not. Maybe I'll just ask him outright. All this sneaking around behind people's backs is tiring."

"I do have some news that will cheer Belle up though," replied Georgie.

"What's that?"

"Dr Lily is happy to help out at the Pet Expo so we'll both be there on the day with our supplies to jab all the little cats and dogs."

"That's great, Belle will be so pleased."

Lucy was smiling as she hung up the phone and dialled the number for Kate in Maintenance. Kate answered promptly and the next ten minutes were very productive. Not only did Kate know all the signatories to the Council contracts, but she was also happy to give Lucy the information. All this Council transparency was helpful today.

Armed with names, dates and company details, Lucy did a Google search on each person and narrowed down the possibilities. With the exception of one contract, the rest were long standing. Mark may have signed the contract extensions but it was more rubber stamping than actually making any decisions. It would have been more shocking if he hadn't signed the extensions.

The one exception was the contract for the maintenance of council plants. All the lovely plants throughout the council offices were leased from a garden centre. Once a week the company visited all the council offices to water and maintain the plants. If one plant was not thriving in its position, they would replace it with another species.

This had been a long-standing contract too until the previous company had gone bankrupt. The plants had been removed from the offices as part of the company's liquidation and it had been several months before a replacement supplier had been found.

And the dates tied in. Mark, as the council's representative, had signed the contract with the new garden centre in July at the start of the current financial year and Jane's stock market tips had begun in late August.

Lucy noted all the relevant details including the contract dates. The garden centre had a dedicated key card to open all the council offices which gave access the photocopier room. And different garden centre employees were in the offices tending to the plants on a regular basis so the presence of someone in a garden centre uniform would not have seemed unusual.

The signatory to the contract was Alexander Petras. Petras was the owner of a garden centre chain. The company had a number of outlets throughout South Australia including Mount Gambier, Port Augusta, Whyalla and Port Pirie. Nothing was private these days, in fact companies made an effort to tell potential customers about their history. He had been handed the company by his father and it was still a family concern with his mother and siblings involved in its running. Lucy could find nothing else to link Mark with someone named Petras. There was no reference of a relationship in any of Mark's social medial, nor any random entries on the Internet, so why did that name sound familiar?

chapter thirty-two

As Belle and Kelly finished their private conversation, Jack returned to his desk. Belle immediately took the opportunity to walk to Arthur's desk, raise her voice and ask for the map, "Arthur, time's up. Have you finished the Placement Map?"

"I'm just finalising the last details," Arthur retorted, "I'll give it to you shortly."

Belle glared across to Jack who nodded and joined the conversation, "Arthur, can you please give Belle whatever you've done."

"Why can't I finish it?"

"Because you were supposed to finish it last week. I gave you ample opportunity but now just give it to Belle."

"Humpf," Arthur grumbled and gave Belle the folder he was holding.

She looked inside and there was the Placement Map. It was all completed with sites allocated to exhibitors, suppliers, vets, people food and drink and even a spot assigned for the toilets. Arthur had done a good job and Belle grudgingly told him so.

"Why did you make such a big deal about this?" Belle asked, "It's really good. All I need to do is tell everyone where they've been assigned."

"Of course it's good," Arthur replied, "Do you think you're the only one who can do things?"

"No, but you have to admit you've been … difficult about finishing this?"

Jack decided to intervene at this point, "Belle now you have the map, are you okay to contact everyone with all the last details?"

"Yes, I'll send an email to everyone today and that leaves just over two weeks for people to ask any questions."

Arthur left the office in a huff and as the others were returning to their desks, Belle turned and pointedly asked in a loud voice, "Jack you said that you were with Mark on the day of Jane's murder then came back to the office for lunch?"

"Yes. That's what happened." Jack was unexpectedly defensive, obviously not liking discussing this in front of others. But it was exactly what Belle wanted. She was hoping that it would attract the attention of Frank and Kevin and perhaps they would want to join the conversation.

"I'm not doubting you," Belle smiled, "I was only wondering if you saw Mark leave his office? And if you saw which direction he went."

"Uh, well no. I didn't see him leave his office. Where did Mark say he went?"

"He said he had lunch at the Plaza. But no details and I was thinking if you saw Mark leave, that's at least a slight confirmation that he wasn't here killing Jane."

"Sorry," Jack replied, "I came straight back to the office and didn't see anything."

Kevin chose that moment to interject, "Mark was definitely out of his office by about quarter to twelve. I went to see him but he wasn't there."

"Are you sure it was last Tuesday, the day Jane was killed?" Belle pushed.

"It would be hard to forget, apart from the murder, I nearly got run over twice in the same place on the same day," Kevin replied."

"What happened?"

"As I said, I was going to see Mark about taking some leave and as I turned the corner, Paige nearly ran me over. She was in such a rush that she didn't see me until it was nearly too late. She said that she'd been to the toilet."

"That was weird. Why would she tell you she'd been to the toilet?" Frank mused.

"I don't know. But it got me thinking and when Mark wasn't in his office, I decided to go to the same place."

"You went to the Ladies?" laughed Frank.

"Ha ha, you know what I mean. And then on my way back to the office Noah nearly barrelled into me with his trolley. Thankfully the trolley was empty or we could have had a huge mess to clean up. Anyway there was no harm done. Noah went to the lift, I checked Mark's office again and it was still empty."

Belle looked very interested, "So there was about half an hour around 12.00pm where Mark was unaccounted for."

"At least that long," Kevin confirmed, "I didn't stick around looking for him."

"Why all the interest in Marks' movements?" asked Frank.

Belle looked at Frank. Maybe it was time to include a few more people in their search for the murderer? And they'd sort of cleared both Frank and Kevin. It would be nice to get a fresh opinion from someone who knew all the suspects.

"I think Mark might have been involved in Jane's death," Belle pronounced.

Frank didn't seem surprised, "Why do you say that?"

Belle took a gamble and listed off all the evidence stacked against Mark; he was being blackmailed by Jane for stock and taxation information and the blackmailing requests were increasing; if the conflict of interest was discovered, it could have resulted in a scandal and we know how the current Mayor felt about scandals so Mark's job was on the line; and this made his contact a suspect too; perhaps they were in it together and either of them could access the photocopier room.

Belle took another deep breath and continued, "It's possible he was breaking the law with his taxation scheme; his alibi was very flimsy with gaps of time where he could have been in the photocopier room; he was quite callous in how he referred to Jane's death; calling it "fortuitous" for the budget but he could have meant it was lucky for another reason and finally the murderer had little empathy for the office and how it would affect their day to day lives which was typical of Mark."

Frank considered all this information and nodded his head, "It all fits."

"And it fits with what we were saying," Kevin said, "We always wondered why he behaved the way he did after the police arrived."

At Belle's quizzical look, Kevin expanded, "Once the police arrived, Mark made his statement and left. The rest of us at least tried to find out what happened. Mark didn't. And why did he leave without seeing if the rest of us were okay? Even he couldn't be that self-centred without a reason."

Frank continued, "We wondered if he had to leave? Did he have something to hide before the police found it? Did he have to get rid of something?"

Jack had listened to these revelations with much interest and asked, "How did you come to this conclusion? What were your thoughts on the rest of us?"

"If the murderer was one of us, we thought that Mark was the most likely. Hitting someone hard enough to kill them suggested a male rather than a female ..."

"Hey!" Belle objected, "We could do it if we wanted to."

"You'd like to be kept on our list of suspects?" Frank asked, his voice full of sarcasm.

"No," Belle replied, "But it's a pretty sexist way of thinking."

"Keep going Frank," Jack tried to get the conversation back on topic.

"If we eliminate the females in the office, we are left with five males; Mark, you, Arthur, Kevin and me. I knew that I hadn't killed her and I was ninety-nine percent sure that Kevin hadn't either which left Mark, Arthur and you."

"And I knew that I hadn't harmed her," Kevin interjected glaring at Frank, "We thought about the three of you and what sort of people you are. Arthur is just so old fashioned and religious that it would be out of character for him to hit any woman over the head, regardless of how annoying she was being."

"And you ..." Frank stopped, clearly thinking that talking about his boss in this way would not be good for his career.

"Yes, and me?"

"We thought that you are a different generation from Arthur and possibly lack his sense of chivalry. But although Jane was causing you lots of problems, we had trouble picturing you hitting an elderly woman over the head."

"And Mark," Belle asked.

"We could picture him hitting someone to get what he wanted," shrugged Kevin.

"It was more than that," said Frank, "Mark is very focused on his own needs, often to the exclusion of anyone else's. It was strange the way he acted when the police came the first time and it's been unusual how he's

141

behaved since. It's like he wants to forget Jane ever existed and move on with the future. From a character perspective, he's the best fit."

Belle nodded, "We've been looking at motives and opportunity rather than the personalities involved. But you're right, it fits."

Had they found the murderer?

chapter thirty-three

Lucy was met with silence as she approached the Animal Control team. They were contemplating the idea of Mark as the murderer.

"What's wrong?" asked Lucy.

"Nothing," replied Belle, "Frank and Kevin have been explaining why, out of all of us, they think Mark is the person most likely to have thumped Jane. And it makes sense. Now we have motive, opportunity and personality."

"And I found the person who's probably his contact. The guy who owns the company which maintain our plants. It's the only new council contract in the last couple of years and the timing fits with Jane's spreadsheet and when the share market tips started."

"Is there any other link between this guy and Mark?"

"No, nothing I could find. Mark doesn't post about his private life online and if he was doing something dodgy at work, he probably wouldn't put it up either."

"Why are you interested in this plant guy" asked Kevin.

Lucy replied, "We think Mark may have had a partner. And if he was being blackmailed for share tips, his co-conspirator in the stock market venture may be a good point to start."

"Are you saying that Mark had a partner who works in a garden centre?" asked Frank.

"I think so. And he owns the garden centre. It's a family business and he inherited it from his father. Why do you ask?"

"A long time ago, there was a group of us talking about different jobs we'd had before ending up here. I remember Mark talking about working for his mate's father as a labourer in a garden centre."

"Why would you remember that?" asked Belle.

"I was surprised that Mark ever did manual work. Can you imagine him hefting bags of soil and fertiliser around? He's such a lazy bloke" Frank replied, "But if this garden centre chap is the same person, they've been friends for decades."

"Maybe there was something suspicious about the garden centre contract after all. Maybe Mark lied about why Jane was blackmailing him. Maybe he did give the contract to an old friend rather than the best supplier."

"It is a strong motive," Frank replied, "The Mayor has made it abundantly clear that he won't put up with any scandalous behaviour and if someone heard about it, the internet and papers would have a field day."

"Speaking of motives, what's yours?" Belle blurted out.

Frank laughed, "What makes you think I have a motive?"

"You said everybody had secrets including yourself but that you wouldn't kill to cover it up," Belle replied, "So what is it? And where did you go on the day of the murder? It's very convenient that you happened to be absent when Jane was killed."

"I thought we were considering Mark as the main suspect, not me."

"We are, and if we clear up what you were doing, it makes for a stronger case against Mark."

Belle and Frank glared at each other, willing the other to blink first.

"Fine," Frank spat, "If you really want to know, I was at Ballroom's Dance Studio learning how to waltz."

He continued on to explain that his thirtieth wedding anniversary was fast approaching and he wanted to surprise his wife. They had been drifting apart for a while and he had planned a big night to help them reconnect. Unfortunately his wife loved to dance and Frank had two left feet, hence the need for secret dance lessons.

"That's it. Nothing grubby. I wouldn't risk anything messing up my marriage. And my secret is staying a secret. You don't need to know it."

Belle nodded her head, "Thanks Frank."

Although he did not want to disclose his secret, Belle was sure the old gossip about the affair was right but getting Frank to admit that would be nearly impossible. And not really necessary at this point.

"And while we're clearing things up," Lucy interrupted, "Kevin, what's with all the strange auction posts on your Facebook page?"

Kevin blushed, "No-one here was supposed to see them."

"Why does nobody in this office manage their privacy settings properly? Especially with all the computer training we get," Lucy was flabbergasted and turned back to Kevin, "What's the big deal then?"

Hesitantly at first then with more enthusiasm, Kevin explained that his family had owned an auction house until the 1930s when it crashed during the Great Depression. He had grown up listening to his grandfather telling stories of those times. The strange buyers, different sellers plus the weird and wacky items which were sold. Before he died, the pair often searched out unusual auctions both in person and later, when his grandfather became frailer, online. The more unusual the items up for auction, the more interested they were.

Kevin finished with, "I suppose I keep up the tradition for him. I search out unusual auction items for sale and post them on Facebook. It reminds me of better times."

"That's so nice," Lucy gushed, "Your family must be so proud of you.

"Can we get back to Mark now?" Frank interrupted, clearly not comfortable with the direction of the conversation, "What are we going to do?"

"What can we do? All the evidence we have is circumstantial. We can't even go to the police with what we have," replied Belle, "We have a strong motive and the personality for the crime. Perhaps we should concentrate on the means of the murder?"

"From the 'Out of Order' sign and the police investigation, it seems likely that Jane was killed between 12.00pm and 1.00pm. We know from Kevin that he wasn't in his office from 11.45am to 12.15pm and according to Mark, he had lunch at the Plaza between 12.00pm and 1.00pm. Do we know if he had lunch by himself or did he meet someone?"

Everyone was shrugging their shoulders.

"Who's going to volunteer to ask him about his lunch? Whether he was by himself? Or if someone else joined him?" asked Belle.

There was a lot of looking down at their own knees before Jack said, "I'll do it. I'll ask him for a recommendation for somewhere to eat over at the Plaza and tie it in with that."

Paige, who had been silent until this point, asked, "Why are you doing this? The police made it obvious they think I was responsible even if I haven't heard from them in a couple of days."

145

Lucy walked over to Paige and gave her a quick hug, "You might have strange friends and have trouble telling everything, but we don't think you killed Jane. We don't desert our friends even when they do dumb things."

"Can I help?" Paige asked.

"If Jack checks Mark's alibi, another job is to look into his contact and see if anything pops out, could you do that?"

"Sure. What's the name?"

Lucy shuffled her notes, "Alexander Petras. And he owns the Apollo Garden Centre chain."

Belle was suddenly at attention, "What was that name?"

"Alex Petras."

"Petras is Jennifer King's married name," Belle stated bluntly.

"I knew it sounded familiar," Lucy crowed, "I wonder if there's a link between Mark and Jennifer? She has the best money motive but there was no association between her and anyone in the office so we disregarded her as a suspect. Now I think we need to go looking for a connection."

Their suspect pool had suddenly increased from one to three; from Mark to Mark, his "Petras" contact and possibly Jennifer "Petras".

Adelaide was often considered a small town and this was just further proof.

chapter thirty-four

N ow she had her hands on the completed Placement Map, Belle spent the afternoon composing a raft of emails advising each of the cooks, the testers, the vets and the exhibitors where they would be situated on the day of the Pet Expo. Only two and a bit more weeks and it would be show time.

Looking at her 'to do list' Belle was happy to note that everything was on track. If all the winning cooks sent in their recipes, including ingredients and equipment, by the end of next week as requested, they could be checked and all the required supplies purchased the following week.

On the documentation front, only the guides being updated by Frank and Kevin were outstanding. Belle wondered how many alterations she would need to make.

"Frank, Kevin, are the guides we discussed last week ready for printing?" Belle called out across the office.

"They're on the group drive," Frank replied smugly, "All ready to go."

Kevin walked over to Belle's desk and dropped off a copy of each guide, "Here's a copy of both."

"Thank you," Belle picked up the 'Guide for new pet owners' and checked it. A section on snakes and rats had been added as she'd asked and the range of choices open for pet owners had been expanded to show the wide options available now. Belle put down the 'Guide for new pet owners' and picked up the 'How to combat barking dogs' guide.

The 'How to combat barking dogs' brochure had needed more updating than the 'Guide for new pet owners' and as Belle leafed through the guide, she found the changes made were very thorough. As well as the standard tips for managing barking dogs, many other options had been researched and included.

Belle walked over to Frank and Kevin's desks, holding the copies of the guides, "Guys, you've done a great job with these. Thank you so much."

"You're welcome," replied Kevin while Frank smiled and nodded his head.

"Who's done a great job? And with what?" asked Mark, appearing quietly in the office.

There was an uncomfortable silence as everyone hoped someone else would answer.

Belle finally found her voice and replied, "Kevin and Frank have been updating these guides for the Pet Expo and have done a wonderful job."

"Well done," Mark directed his thanks at Frank and Kevin, who didn't know where to look.

"They are the last documents we needed to start printing for the expo. Kelly has the afternoon off, her kids have their end of year graduation today, but I'll have her do all the printing tomorrow or Monday and that will be another Pet Expo job completed," Belle continued.

"How is the Pet Expo shaping up?" asked Mark, "With all the drama that's being going on, I haven't taken much notice lately."

Jack chose that moment to join them, "It's going really well Mark."

"Good, good, good."

"I'm meeting some people for lunch at the Plaza next week and I'm looking for a recommendation. You had lunch there last week, didn't you? Where did you go?" Jack asked Mark.

"We had lunch at the little Italian place near the Cinemas," replied Mark, always willing to swagger.

"Was the food good? Price okay? Is it suitable for a group of people?"

"It was only the two of us and it was fine. It might be a bit noisy if there's a crowd of you trying to speak. Being Greek, my friend isn't too keen on Italian food but he loves pizza and they do make a good pizza for a reasonable price."

"Was that Alexander Petras you had lunch with? I heard someone saw him around here."

"Do you know Alex?" Mark asked cautiously.

"No, someone just mentioned seeing him in the building. He must have been here to meet you for lunch."

"No, we met at the restaurant," Mark replied brusquely, "They must have been mistaken."

Mark turned away and walked to where Lucy was cleaning up in the reception area.

"Lucy, are you available for a meeting tomorrow morning at 10.00am?"

"Sure, what's it about?"

"Jennifer King, Jane's daughter is coming in to sign some papers with Human Resources and then is meeting with me to finalise Jane's employment. I thought it would be beneficial if another woman was at the meeting."

****

"And he had no idea how sexist he was being. Thinking that having another woman present would make the murder all better, stupid man," Lucy ranted to Belle and Paige later that night.

Paige had spent time during the afternoon digging into the social media for both Alexander Petras and the Apollo Garden Centre chain. When she approached Lucy to pass on her discoveries, Lucy invited her for dinner to ensure they weren't overheard.

"But hopefully it will give me the chance to ask Jennifer a few questions," Lucy concluded her tirade about Mark's meeting.

After a simple dinner of chicken and salad, the three colleagues were sitting in the loungeroom. Cooper had taken his normal place curled up next to Belle who absentmindedly scratched his ears while listening to Lucy fume. If Mark was the killer, then his sexist attitude was the least of his problems.

"Do we have definite proof that Alexander Petras and Jennifer Petras are related?" Belle asked Paige.

"If we take photos on websites as proof, then yes, they're family," Paige confirmed, "I checked the Apollo Garden Centre chain website and found many photos which identified Alexander Petras as the owner. Then I looked at Jennifer's Facebook, and while most of the posts were of the kids doing crafty things, there were enough photos of the family group to confirm that Alexander Petras is her husband and father of the kids."

"That raises quite a few questions; like why didn't she mention that her husband's company maintained the office plants where her Mum was killed;

and that he knew Mark, at least from a business sense if not from childhood if Frank is to be believed; and then she probably knows Mark too," Belle conjected.

"All good questions. Now Jennifer has a possible accomplice or maybe even two, she must be a plausible suspect. She inherits everything and we know that there's at least $20,000 involved. And that's only the money motive. She also could have been trying to protect her husband and his shady deal with Mark and the council. And we know she didn't get on with her Mum."

"What do we do now?" asked Paige reaching for another chocolate biscuit.

"Mark is meeting with Jennifer tomorrow and I'll be there. The conversation will have to touch on Jane's murder and that will give me the chance to ask some questions," replied Lucy.

"I'm hoping to finish up all the Pet Expo documents tomorrow but I could help afterwards?" offered Belle.

"I could help too," offered Paige.

"Let's wait and see what comes from the meeting. Then we can plan our next steps," replied Lucy, "Maybe we could have lunch?"

This was met with general agreement and the chatter turned to comparing contestants on the latest reality TV show.

Sometimes escaping into reality TV was the best option when real life was overwhelming.

chapter thirty-five

10.00am came very early the following morning. Lucy walked to Mark's office with mixed feeling of excitement and trepidation. If she managed to ask the right question, the mystery may be solved that day. If she asked the wrong question, danger may follow.

Mark and Lucy made small talk while waiting for Jennifer King to arrive. The shadow of previous conversations was apparent; Mark was cautious remembering his earlier disclosures; Lucy was guarded because of their disturbing findings.

"Hi Mark," Jennifer greeted Mark as she entered his office.

Mark stood and gestured to a nearby chair, "Hi Jennifer, did you get everything sorted with Human Resources?"

"Yes," she sighed, "Hopefully that's the end of it."

Lucy cleared her throat.

"Oh yes, Jennifer this is Lucy Anderson," Mark introduced the women. Jennifer nodded hello.

"When HR said you were meeting with them, I thought you may like to see where your Mum worked and … umm … where it happened. Lucy found your Mum and could give you more details if you are interested?"

"Are you crazy?" Jennifer stood up, "I thought you wanted me to sign papers or pick up personal belongings. Not that you wanted me to be ghoulish and stare at where she died. Have you got all the blood stains preserved, just waiting for me to come? Idiot."

She picked up her handbag and left the office. Lucy immediately got up and followed her into the corridor.

"Jennifer, don't leave like this," Lucy consoled, "Let's go and get a cup of coffee and you can tell me how stupid Mark is?"

Jennifer smiled, "He really is an idiot. And I would like a drink before heading home."

Lucy led her to the staffroom and got coffee and biscuits for both of them before sitting down at a table tucked in a corner.

"I didn't know that you and Mark were friends?" Lucy asked.

"What makes you think we are friends?" Jennifer replied from behind her coffee cup.

"For starters, when you walked into his office, you didn't introduce yourself and he knew who you were," Lucy said, "And it's rare for strangers to call each other 'idiot', at least to their face."

"Mark has been friends with my husband since they were kids," Jennifer admitted.

"Why didn't you tell Belle when you were talking to her?"

"The police knew but I didn't see it was any of her business. And today when it became clear that Mark hadn't told you, I decided to follow his lead. That is, until you asked me directly."

"Were the police interested in your relationship with Mark?" Lucy asked, "I mean it does open up the possibility of collusion."

"You think Mark and I planned to kill my Mother? Why would I do that?"

"While we were looking for the work permits, we found reference to savings totalling around $20,000. That is a decent sum of money which gives you a monetary motive as her beneficiary."

Jennifer laughed, "$20,000? I normally don't like to talk about money or our financial standing but this is different. $20,000 is not a lot of money for me or for my family. Look at me."

Lucy did look at Jennifer. She was very well dressed, accessorised with premium solid gold jewellery and an engagement ring where the diamond had to be at least two carats. And was that a Birkin Bag at her feet? They cost serious money. If Jennifer could afford to buy a Birkin Bag, perhaps she was telling the truth about not needing Jane's money.

"Okay, if you don't need the money, then maintaining your family's reputation could be another possible motive," Lucy countered.

"How is my family's reputation at stake?"

"Did you know that your husband and Mark have a contract whereby his company maintains the plants for the council?"

"Yes, I was part of putting the Bid document together. How is that a problem?"

"Since Mark kept his relationship with your husband secret, there's been some talk about whether the contract is a bit shady? Especially when we found out that Jane was blackmailing Mark so he would help her with the stock market."

Jennifer started laughing, "Mum wasn't blackmailing Mark in the traditional sense, even if he grumbles about it like that."

"What was happening then?" asked Lucy.

"My husband, Alex, and Mark have been friends since they were kids and as teenagers, they did some crazy teenager things. Unfortunately as they've aged, they have retained that part of their brains where stupid things sound eminently sensible after a few drinks."

"Been there."

"After the contract between Apollo Garden Centre and the council was signed, Alex and Mark went out for a celebratory drink. Several hours later, Alex rang me at the hotel where we were staying and asked me to pick him and Mark up from Civic Park and bring towels. So I did. I found both men wet and bedraggled, sitting on a park bench. Apparently they had decided that the occasion should be celebrated by their rendition of the Zorba the Greek dance in the fountain."

Lucy started giggling, "I would like to have seen that."

"Me too. And guess who did?"

"Jane was there? She saw them?"

"Yes. When I got there, Mark was in a panic. She'd taken a video on her phone before she went home and had threatened or teased him that she'd show everyone at work."

"What was she doing there?" asked Lucy.

Jennifer shrugged her shoulders, "No idea, there were a few people around, some heading home from the cinema complex across the road, others from dinner, and she happened to be one of them. Just bad luck for the guys. Anyway, the rest of the story is that the next day Mark offered to help Jane with some stock market tips if she'd keep quiet about them dancing in the fountain."

"That explains the timing of the tips with the signing of the contract," Lucy replied, "I wonder why he is still giving Jane information after all this time?"

"Mark likes to show off his expertise and have people looking up to him," Jennifer said, "And if Mum was telling people that his tips were good, he's probably prancing around like a peacock."

"You may be right," Lucy smiled, "Did Mark know that Jane was your Mum?"

"I don't think so," Jennifer said, "As I told Belle on the phone, I haven't seen or spoken to Mum in a very long time. I knew she had worked at the council and I knew Mark worked there too. I didn't realise until Mark was telling this story that they worked together. Alex realised then too but he didn't say anything. He thought it was up to me if I decided to tell Mark."

"Didn't Alex recognise Jane on the night?"

"He was too plastered to recognise his own mother, let alone a woman he'd only met a couple of times many years ago."

"Why do you think Mark is keeping his relationship with Alex quiet then, especially if the contract is genuine?

"No idea why, the contract is definitely legitimate. I've been part of Bid Proposal Teams for quite a few of these contracts and there was nothing different. Our company is competitive; our pricing and service schedules are in line with the going market rates. Plus Alex and Mark's friendship was even identified in the contract to avert any claims of favouritism."

"If the contract is valid and Jane wasn't really blackmailing Mark, our prime suspect is in the clear," Lucy reasoned, "Unless of course, you know someone else who wanted to kill your mother?"

"I don't know if he wanted to kill her but Harry Rossi possibly had a reason."

"Who's Harry Rossi?" asked Lucy.

"He's the main beneficiary of Mum's will."

"But I thought it all went to you? You said that $20,000 wasn't a lot of money for you."

"No, I get $10,000 and Harry Rossi gets the rest."

"Who is he? Did she have a boyfriend that we didn't know about?" Lucy sounded flabbergasted.

"No idea who he is. I'd never heard the name before the lawyers contacted me but, as you know, Mum and I weren't close. He could be a boyfriend or just a friend or a neighbour or anybody really."

"How much money do you think he will inherit?"

"You said there was $20,000 somewhere so he will inherit at least $10,000 when it's found. I haven't started looking at all her papers yet. I'm taking them home and as Executor will sort through everything in the next couple of weeks."

Lucy was surprised at the lack of urgency shown by Jennifer. If the positions had been reversed, Lucy would already have those papers in separate piles for payment, cancellations, general notifications and filing. Maybe this was harder for Jennifer than she was letting on. Her reluctance to talk details and progress the probate was understandable; it had only been ten days and this was only the first time they'd met, even if Lucy had been researching Jennifer for over a week.

Maybe Jane had another secret they hadn't discovered.

Before leaving Jennifer, Lucy made arrangements to send Jane's laptop to Whyalla. Surprisingly, Jennifer decided that she would like to see her Mum's gambling spreadsheet although she had no idea what she would do with it. With Jane's house keys already having been returned to her landlord, there was no need for any further contact with Jennifer. Lucy felt it was the start of the final chapter to Jane's life.

On her way back to her desk, Lucy stopped at Mark's office. She reassured him that Jennifer was okay and on her way back to Whyalla.

"Why didn't you say that you knew Jane's daughter and that you were friends?" Lucy asked.

"It was only after Jane was killed that Alex, Jen and I worked out all the intricacies of who was who. The police knew but we decided to keep it quiet to avoid confusion unless someone asked directly and I'm guessing that's what you did."

Lucy nodded, "But didn't you see Jane at the wedding? According to what Jennifer told Belle, that's when all the trouble between them really blew up."

"When Alex married Jen, I was stuck overseas and couldn't get to the wedding. I heard about the ruckus Jen's Mum caused after I got back but didn't tie it to our Jane."

"And why didn't you say that you knew Alex when the contract was being signed?"

"Our friendship was noted in the contract but I didn't make a big deal about it. I've known Alex nearly my whole life, Alex's Dad even gave me my first job, and I didn't want people to think that he was getting the council contract through favouritism. His company's bid really was the best one.

"And is that why you were always vague about your Plaza lunch alibi??

"Apollo Garden Centres are a big, successful company which the council is lucky to be involved with. There have been takeover rumblings and the last thing they need is to be linked to a murder investigation so I tried to keep my friend out of it. What's so bad about that?"

"Looking out for your friend is understandable but why did you just leave us after Jane had been killed? You spoke to the police and left with no thought about any of us," Lucy ventured.

"I am sorry about that. While I was waiting for the police to come and interview us, I rang Alex to let him know because he was my alibi. That's when we found out Jen's Mum and Jane were the same person because the police had contacted them already. We decided on the phone, not to say anything until we'd had a chance to discuss it. We knew that it could look bad."

"So you left?" Lucy asked.

"You, of all people, know that I'm useless at keeping my mouth shut without a solid plan. I thought the best thing to do was to go home, ring Alex from there and make a plan."

"Okay. But why did you leave those envelopes for me to deliver urgently? It left the front desk vacant from 12.00 noon until nearly 12.30pm on the day of the murder. Which meant I couldn't see if anyone unusual entered the photocopier room or at least the hallway leading to it. Did you mean to get me out of the way?"

Mark looked abashed, "Nothing so sinister I'm afraid. In the envelopes were copies of a report that I was supposed to distribute by last week but I'd forgotten to do. By sending hard copies rather than an email, it gave me a valid reason why the reports were late."

"All this means is that there's nothing suspicious about your friendship with Alex and Jennifer, the plant maintenance contract is legitimate, you didn't arrange for the front desk to be vacant and that you didn't kill Jane."

"Right on all counts."

****

"Mark, Alex and Jennifer are all cleared," Lucy announced dramatically to Belle, Paige and Kelly across the staffroom table, "But we have a new suspect."

When Lucy returned from Mark's office, Belle and Paige were waiting to go to lunch. As they prepared to leave, Kelly asked where they were going and then invited herself as well. The women had an hour to eat and chat before they needed to return to their desks and allow Frank, Kevin and Arthur to leave for lunch.

Lucy went on to explain Mark's reasons for keeping his friendship with Alex and Jennifer quiet, why he was passing stock information to Jane and why he deserted the team on the day of the murder. She also spoke about Jennifer's wealth and lack of need for Jane's money. Her description of the Birkin Bag was long and detailed.

"But it looks like we have another 'other' to investigate," Lucy had saved the best for last, "Jane left nearly everything to a guy named Harry Rossi."

"What? I thought she left it all to Jennifer?" Kelly exclaimed.

Lucy repeated what Jennifer had told her, "And she hadn't ever heard of this bloke. Do any of you know the name?"

There was a general shaking of heads while this news sunk in.

"Did Jane have a boyfriend?" asked Belle.

"Not that Jennifer knew about," replied Lucy, "Paige you sat closest to her, did you ever hear anything that might suggest she was seeing someone?"

"No. Jane was very private, she didn't really speak about her life outside of work. She didn't make personal phone calls from here. I actually didn't think she had much of a life. I was even surprised to hear you say she was buying shares from Mark's tips. She never said anything about that."

Lucy explained what they'd found in Jane's home. The Las Vegas dream, the shares, the horseracing, the scratchies and all the gambling spreadsheets. Both Paige and Kelly were dumbfounded.

"How could we not know about something so big?" asked Kelly.

"While Jane was loud about everything she heard and saw here, she did keep her personal life quiet," Lucy said, "That's how she might've had a secret boyfriend that we knew nothing about."

As the women contemplated this possibility imagining Jane sneaking around with a man. But why would she have been sneaking? She wasn't married or seeing anyone else, as far as they knew anyway. Was it Jane just keeping everything to herself or was there a more sinister reason? And if so, what sort of reason could it be?

"We need to find out more about this guy," Belle stated the obvious, "Do we know anything else about him?"

"No," replied Lucy, "I was so surprised when Jennifer said she wasn't the sole heir, I forgot to ask anything apart from his name and how much he got."

"How do we find him?" asked Paige.

"Our friend Georgie is pretty good with social media; we could start there?"

"But if this guy is about Jane's age, how likely is it that he will have any social media?"

"Umm. Good point. Jane didn't really have any."

"What about trying the White Pages? Don't older people still have landlines and be listed in the telephone directory?" suggested Kelly.

Belle looked at Lucy, "I think Mum and Dad are still in the White Pages even though they have mobiles and that's how we ring them."

"And they're just a bit older than Jane," Lucy agreed.

"It's worth a try," said Belle, "But don't get your hopes up; there might a hundred of them listed. Harry Rossi is a pretty common name."

"I know that name," said a deep voice from behind Belle.

chapter thirty-seven

I know that name," said Frank as he approached the staffroom table, "I used to work here with a guy named Harry Rossi."

"Did you?"

"Where is he now?"

"How long ago?"

"Did Jane know him?"

The questions pelted Frank as he sat down with his lunch, "Yes I worked with a bloke called Harry Rossi about twenty years ago. We were both Parking Inspectors back then. Where is he now? I don't know. We lost touch when I moved on. It's a shame really, we were good mates back then. He was a few years older than me if I remember right but we were both married with young kids so we had quite a bit in common."

Frank gazed into the distance recalling earlier days and how much had happened and how much had changed since.

"And did Jane know him?" Lucy repeated her question.

"How would I know?" asked Frank, "She would have been with the Council then so it's possible I guess."

"I hate to point it out, but we don't know anything about the Harry Rossi that's in Jane's will," Kelly interjected, "He might only be twenty years old or could live in Queensland for all we know."

"What do you mean by Jane's will?" asked Frank just as Kevin sat down at the staffroom table.

"Lucy, you explain to Frank and Kevin while the rest of us go back to work," said Belle as she rose to leave the lunch area, "We can think of some ideas for finding him during the afternoon."

Belle, Kelly and Paige left Lucy, Frank and Kevin discussing the latest developments. Arthur had obviously decided to lunch elsewhere if his absence was any guide while Jack was still in a meeting in the city Council office.

Lucy repeated the gist of her conversations with both Jennifer and Mark to Frank and Kevin, "To summarise, Mark is just an idiot who tried to keep innocent things quiet and Jennifer is the executor of Jane's will but not the primary beneficiary."

"And this Harry Rossi inherits most of the money?" asked Frank.

"Yep."

"And the only thing you know about him is his name?" asked Kevin.

"Yep."

"What are you going to do now?" asked Frank.

Lucy gave a big sigh, "First we need to find out who he is. Then we need to find out if he has an alibi for the time of the murder. And then I suppose we need to find out if he killed Jane."

Kevin scratched his face, "Did you ask the daughter if she had any contact information for him? The lawyer who drew up the will must know his address or phone number and if she's executor, surely she has it now too?"

"Belle suggested the same thing. I'll ring Jennifer later and ask."

"Why not ring her now?"

"She was leaving to drive home and she's unlikely to know the details off by heart. I'll ring her in a couple of hours when she's had the chance to get to Whyalla."

"In the meantime, I'll check the Council's database and see if a Harry Rossi still works here," replied Frank.

Lucy left Frank and Kevin to eat their lunches and debate the latest information.

Later that afternoon Lucy picked up the phone to call Jennifer. She was a bit apprehensive. Jennifer had been lovely this morning but maybe she would think Lucy was crossing a line.

"Hi Jennifer, it's Lucy Anderson; we met this morning?"

"Oh, hello," she replied, "What can I do for you?"

"This may sound strange but I was wondering if you had any other information about Harry Rossi? A phone number or maybe an address? And what was the date of the will?"

"I do but why should I give it to you?" Jennifer was starting to sound annoyed.

"I'm trying to discover who killed your mother. I would have thought that you'd want to help in any way you could?"

"This is a job for the police; not her nosy work colleagues," retorted Jennifer, "You're not the main suspect anymore so why are you still investigating?"

Lucy was rendered silent. Why were they continuing to investigate? Sure Paige was under consideration by the police but Sgt Harris had shown that he was looking at everyone so she should be fine. Paige and Kelly had been good sounding boards today. Jack had helped Belle earlier in the week. Even Frank and Kevin were excited to be part of the investigation.

"I don't exactly know why we're still investigating," Lucy admitted to Jennifer, "But I do know that in a weird way this investigation is helping the office grieve."

Lucy continued, "Our office has been struggling before this happened and maybe your Mum's death is somehow bringing us all together. Everyone seems to be aiming towards one goal; to find who killed Jane. And for me, there will always be an element of doubt in these relationships until we find the culprit."

"I suppose that makes some sort of sense," Jennifer begrudgingly replied.

"That's why we're still trying to discover what happened," said Lucy, "But I am puzzled why you aren't trying at all?"

It was Jennifer's turn to be silent.

"The easy answer is our estrangement but I think it's more than that," Jennifer started, "There is a mixture of regret and guilt. When I first got the news, my first feeling was anger. She was so horrible and I really wished that we could have had a better mother-daughter relationship. And when she was gone, the chance for reconciliation had vanished."

"I'm sorry," Lucy said.

"Did you know she rang me the week before she died?" Jennifer continued, "But I didn't take the call or bother to return it. Now I'll always wonder why she rang."

Lucy stayed quiet as Jennifer pondered this impossibility.

"You're right. We need to try all angles to find this person. Hold on while I find the information."

Jennifer returned quickly and gave the details to Lucy, "The will was only dated a couple of weeks ago too. Could you please let me know if you find anything out? And of course if I can help in any way."

Lucy finished the phone call with a mixture of sadness and eagerness; she had the details of their next lead.

chapter thirty-eight

G ot it," Lucy announced as she approached Frank and Kevin's desks.

"Harry Rossi's contact details?" asked Frank.

Lucy nodded.

"What's the address?" asked Frank.

"It's over in Modbury North so it's close," Lucy replied, "And the will was dated just before she died."

"I looked at the Council database and there is a Harry Rossi still working in the Parking Inspections area. Did she give you his phone number?"

"Yes. But only a mobile number so there's no way to know if it's the same person. What should we do?"

"Let's just call the mobile number and see who answers?" suggested Frank.

"And what are you going to say? Are you going to ask whoever answers why Jane left him the money or just if he killed her?" said Kevin.

"Why don't we ring the work number for the Harry Rossi here then?"

"And what are you going to say to him? Same questions?" Kevin rolled his eyes.

"What do you suggest then? We have these phone numbers; do we use them or not?" grumbled Frank.

All three considered the available options and Kevin was the first with an idea, "Maybe you should ring the work number and invite Harry out for a drink saying you've been thinking about the old days and would like to catch up. Then you could meet him at a pub somewhere and see if he is the Harry Rossi from Jane's will."

"That's a good idea," replied Frank, "And I could make it that old sports bar up the road. The old Harry was always having a punt on some horse or another."

Lucy's ears pricked up with the mention of gambling on horses, "Guys did we tell you that we found all this evidence of gambling at Jane's house? It seems she was trying to win enough money for a holiday in Las Vegas. Did she ever mention anything to you?"

Both men shook their heads.

"Shall we give this a go?" asked Kevin.

"Sure," said Frank picking up his office phone and looking at the details on his computer.

Frank dialled the number and waited. After several rings a quietly spoken voice answered, "Parking Inspection, Harry Rossi speaking."

"Hey Harry, it's Frank. Frank Morgan from a long time ago, how are you mate?"

"Frank, how are you? It's been years since we spoke."

"Yeah the years have certainly flown by," Frank said, "What's happening with you these days?"

"Nothing much; good and bad like everyone I suppose. How can I help you?"

"I was just talking to the guys here about the old days and thought it might be nice to catch up and have a beer. What do you think?"

"Actually that would be nice. It seems that everyone around here gets younger every day and it would be nice to chat to someone who knows what it was like before. When were you thinking?"

"How about tomorrow? We could meet at The Arena, that old sports bar up the road, say 2.00pm?"

"That sounds great."

"Okay. My mobile number is 0400 111 222 in case anything happens and you need to contact me," said Frank hopefully.

"Good idea. My number is 0400 987 654. I'll see you tomorrow. I'm really glad you called."

"See you tomorrow."

Frank put the phone down with a flourish, "And that's how it's done. What was the number for the Harry Rossi in the will?"

"0400 987 654."

"We have a match. Parking Inspector Harry Rossi is the same person as Will Harry Rossi. Now we just need to find out how he knew Jane and if he killed her. That shouldn't be too hard," said Frank.

"Good job," said Kevin, "Get a few drinks into him and we should know everything by tomorrow afternoon."

Lucy stared at them. Did they not realise how hard it is to get information from someone? Especially in a murder case. Did they think the man was just going to confess because he'd had a couple of beers?

"Have you got a plan how you are going to get the information?" asked Lucy.

"I'll just ask," replied Frank.

"And if he doesn't answer?"

"Of course he'll answer. Why wouldn't he?"

"And you were willing to share your secrets immediately?" Lucy reminded Frank.

Kevin laughed at Frank's discomfort.

"Umm. Maybe you're right. What do you suggest?"

Lucy started sharing the different things they'd learned when trying to find out information. That having a plan was a good idea. Know what information they wanted to find out. Be prepared to go in a different direction if it happened. Be prepared for different reactions such as anger, defiance, sorrow and delight. And understand that people may react in these different ways for different reasons.

"It's also a good idea to have an answer prepared for the inevitable 'why do you want to know' question," Lucy finished.

"It can't be that hard," said Frank.

"Not for you," replied Kevin rolling his eyes again, "You are a master interrogator and everyone will bow to your questioning."

"Alright," Frank glared at him, "Let's make a plan. First thing, what do we want to know?"

"We want to know how he knew Jane? How they met? How long had they known each other? Were they friends or a couple or something else?" replied Lucy.

"And we want to know why she left him all her money," said Kevin.

"Obviously," Frank was still glaring as he wrote down all the questions.

"Then we need to concentrate on her murder," continued Lucy, "Where was he at the time she was killed and did he have a motive to kill her."

"But we already know his motive; her inheritance," said Kevin.

Frank replied, "But what if he's rich, like Jane's daughter, and doesn't need the money? We'll need to find out if there was any other reason for him wanting her dead. Like if he was her partner, he might have killed her because she dumped him."

"Why would she have kept him in her will if she'd dumped him?" asked Kevin.

"He could be one of those guys who get lonely women to pay for everything then once the woman has changed their will in his favour, he kills them to get the inheritance."

"Anyway," Lucy tried to get back on topic, "We do need to discover any other possible motives."

"The cop shows on TV always talk about Means, Motive and Opportunity," said Kevin, "Motive we have covered, when we find out his alibi that will tell us opportunity but what about means?"

"Everyone pretty much has means with this murder," replied Frank, "They just had to get into the photocopier room and use the stapler that was there."

"Now you know what information we need, what are you going to do if he becomes evasive or even angry?" asked Lucy.

"I'd let it go, have another drink and then try again in a while, maybe asking in a different way," said Kevin.

"I'd keep pushing until he answered the question. He's got nothing to hide unless he killed her," said Frank.

"Maybe he does have something to hide that is nothing to do with Jane's murder and by pushing him you get him really mad and he leaves without telling you anything," countered Kevin.

Lucy made a suggestion with a smile, "Why don't you both go? That way if Frank becomes too Frank-like, Kevin can rein you in."

"Is that okay with you?" asked Kevin, "I would really like to go."

"Yeah, it's probably a good idea," conceded Frank, "What say I pick you up about 1.45pm tomorrow?"

Lucy looked relieved, "One last thing to prepare. What will you say if he asks 'why do you want to know'? Belle and I have gotten burned a couple of times by not preparing a response to this."

"Why don't we just say that we're interested because she was our work colleague?" Frank suggested.

"That sounds like a good answer," replied Kevin, "And we probably need to think about how we're going to ask the other questions."

As Lucy walked back to her desk leaving them to their planning, she thought to herself, "This exercise is either going to be an unmitigated disaster or a glorious triumph." And she wasn't sure which way it was leaning.

chapter thirty-nine

Lucy was sitting at the kitchen table when Belle and Cooper emerged from their cocoon.

"Morning," said Lucy, "Did you sleep well?"

"Morning. Slept off and on I suppose. I wonder how Frank and Kevin are feeling today."

"I think it's worse for us."

"Why?"

"There's nothing we can do; just wait and see what happens. It would be easier if we were out talking to people rather than sitting here."

"But it's also nice to have a day off without murder being the priority. What do you want to do?"

"I don't know. I'd like to recharge but I'm having trouble switching off. I feel a sense of urgency. People at work are reacting more strangely the longer this goes unsolved, starting to look at each other and wonder. There's nothing obvious; just a sense of discomfort or mistrust."

"We need to stay positive. Maybe the guys will get lucky today and it will all be over. We just need to hold on," said Belle, "Hey, I've got an idea. Let's go and have a pedicure and get our toes painted. That will relax us plus we'll have nice toes."

Lucy cheered up, "As long as we get Christmas colours; red or green."

"Sure, I'll get red and you get green."

"But I want red."

"Okay, we'll both get red."

"But who'll get green?"

"Lucy!"

"Thanks Belle."

****

Frank woke late, kissed his wife absently on the cheek and hopped into the shower. He'd had a good night's sleep and was looking forward to catching up with an old mate and talking about the early years. If the mate turned out to be the murderer, at least he would have been involved in solving the mystery.

Kevin, on the other hand, had not slept well. He was more thoughtful than Frank and the many ways this exercise could back-fire kept playing on his mind in a loop. Harry Rossi could get angry, very angry. They were after all snooping in his private business. Or it could be a colossal waste of time. Either Harry knew nothing related to the murder or refused to tell them. Another scenario playing on Kevin's mind was the one where Harry confessed to everything. And while that sounded good, it raised the issue of what to do next. Take him to the police? Let him turn himself in? And what if he takes off?

Frank punctually picked up Kevin at 1.45pm and they entered The Arena. Frank glanced around but couldn't see anyone that looked like his memory of Harry. They went to the bar and ordered a couple of beers and sat down at a nearby table.

The pub was reminiscent of earlier times too. Unlike many up-market bars, rather than floorboards, there was carpet on the floor which lessened the noise from patrons. Although the requisite pokies and high-definition TVs made up for it. The décor was a little dark and dingy but large comfortable chairs for viewing your chosen sport, good basic pub food and reasonable drinks made this a popular place for many.

Right on 2.00pm a short, dumpy man with grey wispy hair entered the pub. He looked around, saw Frank and waved.

"Hey Frank, it's been too long," enthused Harry.

"Yeah it has," said Frank standing to shake his hand, "This is Kevin, he works with me now."

All three men exchanged handshakes before Harry went off to the bar.

"He seems okay," commented Kevin.

"He was a nice guy when I worked with him. But he looks so much older than when I last saw him. I wonder if this is normal or if Jane's death is the cause."

Harry shortly pulled up a chair at the table and asked, "How's everything with you these days? It seems so long ago and we were so young. How's your wife and kids?"

"Erica is well. We're celebrating our thirtieth anniversary this year. The kids are all grown up now. Pippa is working as a lawyer in Sydney and Sam is working in IT in Melbourne. Pippa is engaged to a nice fellow so Erica's hoping for some grandkids soon but Sam is still very single. How's your wife and kids? You had three boys if I remember correctly?"

"Mary died nearly ten years ago."

"I'm sorry, I didn't know," replied Frank.

"No, we'd lost touch by then," Harry said, "It was a long time ago. But the kids are great. Matthew, Mark and Luke. I still see them each week. We have a big family lunch every Sunday with their wives and kids. I have five grandkids now with a new one on the way."

Harry brought out his phone and proudly showed photos of his grandkids. Then Frank brought out his phone and showed his photos. Kevin had sat quietly all this time but decided to get to the point of the afternoon.

"How's work going? Frank said you work in the Parking Inspection section," asked Kevin.

"Work's okay. Nothing seems to change much except technology. Everyone still has the same excuses for parking violations. But my job's secure and that's a good thing in the current climate. How long have you worked with Frank? And Frank where did you end up?" replied Harry.

"Kevin and I have worked together for ages," said Frank, "We work in Animal Awareness and Control."

This statement seemed to startle Harry.

Frank continued, "It's normally pretty calm but the last couple of weeks have been unusual. Did you hear about a council worker being murdered in the office?"

Harry nodded.

"It was one of our colleagues so we've had the police there and everyone being questioned about alibis and motives. Did you know her, Jane King? She's worked for the council for a very long time in different areas, you might have come across her?"

Harry shook his head, "The name is not familiar."

"Maybe you met somewhere else? She was a gambler too. I remember how much you loved to back the horses and she did as well. Maybe you met at a racetrack?"

"No, as I said the name is not familiar. I didn't know her."

Frank glanced at Kevin and the turned to directly face Harry, "If you didn't know Jane, why did her will leave nearly everything to you?"

chapter forty

Harry gulped.

Frank and Kevin waited. Finally Harry replied, "How do you know that?"

"Jane's daughter told us."

"What else do you know?" asked Harry.

"We know when Jane was killed, where it happened and how it happened. We know many different motives for killing Jane and we know lots of people who couldn't have done it. We're narrowing down who could have murdered Jane," said Frank, "Speaking of which, where were you when she died?"

"Me?" asked Harry, "Why ask me for an alibi? I was nowhere near the photocopier room when she died."

"Then how did you know it happened in the photocopier room?"

"It was all over the papers and TV news. Of course I knew."

"And where were you when it happened?"

"Out somewhere. I'm always out and about for my job."

"Can you be more specific?" Kevin asked politely.

"Not now. It was over a week ago. I can check my work diary on Monday and let you know if it's that important."

"Thank you, that would be great," replied Kevin.

"But how did you know Jane?" asked Frank, "Where did you meet? How long have you known her? Were you a couple?"

"That's none of your business," spat Harry getting up to leave as the questions got more personal.

Kevin intervened quickly, "Why don't I buy us another round and we can watch the horses and maybe place a few bets?"

Half an hour later peace had been restored to the table after a couple of rounds had been drunk with some bets won and others lost.

Kevin decided to have another shot, "Jane would have loved this. Did you guys spend time watching the races together?"

Harry apparently was a lightweight drinker, slurring his response, "Yeah, we liked going to the races. Not that we'd been often. We met at work one day last month when her boss sent her across to us to pick up some document or other. Then we saw each other at the races one day and decided to have a drink. Both of us were on our own and it was nice to have some company."

Harry looked into his beer, remembering.

"It was nice to have someone to talk to. My kids are great but they have their own lives. Jane and I could talk freely knowing that because we didn't have anyone in common, nothing would get back to other people in our lives. I could talk about Mary and how much I still missed her without someone telling me to get over it and Jane could talk about her daughter, all the mistakes she'd made and what she was doing to try and fix it."

"We'd only been friends a few weeks but it had been so good for both of us."

'I wonder why Jane didn't say anything at work?" asked Kevin.

"She was a private person. Even in the short time I knew her, she kept a lot to herself. Every time we met I would discover something new about her. But most of the time, it was me doing the talking. Mary has been gone for nearly ten years now and I still miss her every day. Jane was happy for me to tell her all my old stories about the things we did together. My family and old friends have heard these stories many times so it was nice to have someone new to bore. The only thing she really liked to talk about was her daughter. And although it was a very personal subject, I'm guessing she had no-one else to confide in and I could listen without judging."

"Why did you keep your friendship quiet?" said Kevin.

"The first reason was because Jane wanted it kept quiet. For me, I was … concerned how people in my life would react. I pictured being forced into a relationship – everyone likes to matchmake widows and widowers. Plus I didn't want to upset my kids. Jane and I were just friends and we were happy with that but I worried my kids may not like the idea of another woman in my life, even as a friend."

"If you were just friends, why did Jane alter her will to leave the bulk of her estate to you?"

"She only changed her will a couple of weeks ago. Something really good happened and Jane wanted to share it with her daughter. Jane thought it may have been a way to start mending fences. She rang a couple of times but Jennifer wouldn't answer the phone. And when Jane left a message asking Jennifer to call back, she got no response. She was so hurt. I think Jane changed her will out of spite and when she'd calmed down, she'd change it back again. But then she died."

"Leaving you with a whole lot of money?" said Frank.

"More than you think. Jane's good news was buying a winning scratchie. When that ticket is claimed, her estate is going to increase by $100,000."

"$100,000? That gives you a serious motive to kill Jane before she could change her will back," said Frank, "And why you? Why not change it to another family member?"

"I don't think Jane had anyone else to leave it to. She definitely didn't talk about any other family members," replied Harry, "And however much money Jane had, I didn't kill her. And I'll prove it on Monday."

"Where's the winning ticket? No-one's mentioned finding it or the $100,000 if she claimed it," asked Kevin.

"In her Safe Deposit Box," replied Harry.

"She had a Safe Deposit Box?"

"Yeah. Her bank offered different Safe Boxes and Safe Envelopes at their city branch. She kept all of her winnings in the box. She said her winnings were separate from her living money and if it was in a box in the city, she would definitely save it and not spend it on day-to-day expenses. As executor of her will, her daughter will be able to access it once all the paperwork has been arranged."

The next horse race was just about to start and Harry wanted to place a bet. As he walked to the betting counter, Frank and Kevin took big gulps of their drinks.

"Harry's certainly given us a lot of information," commented Kevin.

"And I believe him. He doesn't come across as a killer," replied Frank, "If he can prove he was working at the time of the murder, I think we need to look elsewhere."

"We have answers to all the other questions so let's wait until Monday and see what he shows us and hopefully we can cross him off as a suspect."

Frank nodded his agreement. Harry came back with another round of drinks plus a serve of wedges with sweet chilli sauce and sour cream.

"I thought we could do with some food. Help yourselves," he said, "Do you know what I'll miss most? Jane was saving to go to Las Vegas and when she had enough money, I was going to go with her. We were planning a week in an expensive hotel with good food and drink and lots of gambling."

chapter forty-one

It was Sunday afternoon. Belle and Lucy had returned from the weekly lunch with their folks and were out on the backyard deck with Cooper at their feet. The feet with newly painted toes in bright Christmas red. The weekend had been a nice break from murder. After their pedicures the twins had taken a drive to the beach, paddled in the cool water and eaten fish and chips on the boardwalk.

But now both of them were getting anxious about how Frank and Kevin had fared yesterday. There had been no arrangements for them to report back to the twins before Monday but their patience was running out.

"Are you going to ring him or am I?" asked Belle.

"I assume you're talking about Frank and I will."

Lucy rang Frank's number and turn the phone to speaker mode.

"Hi Frank," said Lucy when he answered, "Belle and I are here on speaker. We're wondering how you went yesterday. Are you able to talk or should we wait until tomorrow?"

"I'm surprised you lasted this long before ringing me," Frank chuckled, "Hold on and I'll get a drink then start talking."

When Frank had his drink organised, he told the twins how the meeting with Harry went yesterday.

He spoke about how Harry had initially denied knowing Jane but when confronted about the will had quickly explained their relationship, how they met though gambling and were only friends. He also repeated what Harry had said about them keeping the relationship quiet.

Frank laughed about how a couple of beers had encouraged Harry to answer whatever questions they asked. He explained Harry's opinion regarding the will being changed through spite and how Harry had expected it to be changed back if she hadn't died. Frank told them about how Jane had been hurt by Jennifer refusing to be in contact with her.

He left the best to last. He repeated Harry's words about the winning $100,000 scratchie ticket and the Safe Deposit Box that no-one had mentioned so far.

"Harry told us he was out of the office for work when Jane died and he's going to check his work diary tomorrow and send proof. Assuming he can do this, I don't think he's a viable suspect. Sure, he has a monetary motive but he didn't sound like a killer and he was sincere in missing Jane."

"Thanks Frank," said Belle, "Good job. It does sound like he's in the clear and I'm thinking we're back to Jennifer again."

"Why?" asked Lucy.

"$10,000 or even $20,000 may not be motive enough for her to have killed her mother but $100,000 is another story."

"But Harry is the heir, not her."

"Not if the money or ticket was to disappear before the contents of the box were handed over to Harry. Remember she is the executor of the will."

Frank and Lucy considered this thought and could raise no valid objections to the idea.

"I guess I'll ring Jennifer tomorrow and see how she reacts to this new information," said Lucy, "It does always seem to come back to her."

****

By the time Lucy arrived at work on Monday, Frank was sitting at his desk. There was a small stack of papers next to his computer which he picked up and waved at Lucy.

"Harry has already sent me an email with photos of his diary entries for the last two weeks. I checked them on screen then printed them out and they look real enough to me. According to these entries, he was on the other side of town on the day of the murder. There was a cross council meeting to discuss standardising some of the parking regulations across Adelaide," said Frank, "It would be easy to verify if he was at that meeting but I still don't think its's him."

Lucy nodded, "I'll ring Jennifer."

Lucy sat at her desk and stared into space. This was a phone call she didn't want to make. She'd already accused this woman only to be shot down and now she was going to do it again. Jennifer still claimed to have an alibi by being in Whyalla at the time her mother died, although they hadn't checked it. The money motive had changed from $20,000 to $100,000 but was that enough money to justify Jennifer killing her mother? Maybe there was another motive they hadn't considered yet? Perhaps Jennifer found out about the changes to the will and was unhappy and lashed out? But how did she get into the photocopier room?

Might as well get this over with, Lucy picked up her phone and dialled the increasingly familiar number. Jennifer answered on the first ring, "Hello."

"Hi Jennifer, it's Lucy Anderson from your Mum's work. You asked to be kept in the loop and we found out some more information over the weekend."

"Great, what did you find?"

"We found Harry Rossi. He was a friend of your Mum's and has a good alibi for the time of her murder. He also explained about the changing of the will and why she tried to ring you before she died."

Jennifer took a deep breath, "Do I want to know?"

"Jane rang you because she'd won some money and thought including you could be the first step to reconciliation," Lucy spoke quietly, "You didn't happen to know about the winning scratchie and the Safe Deposit Box did you? $100,000 is a bit more tempting that $20,000."

"Are you seriously asking me what I think you are asking?"

The volume of Jennifer's voice was steadily rising, "How many times do I have to say that I didn't kill my mother!"

"I'm sorry to keep asking," apologised Lucy, "So many clues keep coming back to you."

"Goodbye," Jennifer coldly replied and hung up the phone.

Another dead end. And they were no closer to finding out who killed Jane.

chapter forty-two

It was morning teatime and nearly everyone was sitting around having a coffee while Lucy repeated the gist of this morning's phone conversation with Jennifer.

"Then who killed Jane?" Paige wailed.

"It looks like no-one here is involved," Lucy said, "We need to start looking for the mysterious 'other'. Any ideas?"

"We could approach her landlord?" suggested Kelly, "You said he searched her place after she died."

"Maybe we should talk to Margaret, her neighbour again?" asked Lucy, "Now she's had time to think, she might have remembered something else?"

"Did you find any outsiders with a motive?" asked Frank, "While it would have been difficult to attack Jane in the photocopier room, it's not impossible if Jane let them in."

"Or did you consider any other council employees? They could easily access the photocopier room," asked Kevin.

"These are all good options," replied Belle, "But we keep finding viable suspects and then clearing them, maybe we should start at the beginning again in case we overlooked anything. Now we have more eyes looking, we might find something that was missed earlier."

"Let's schedule an office meeting tomorrow morning and we can spend an hour or so looking at things from the beginning and hopefully find something to help the police in their enquiries," suggested Jack, hoping that such a meeting might help with office morale as well.

There were general nods of agreement around the table.

After morning tea Lucy headed off for a dentist check-up while Belle and Kelly made a start on the final items on Belle's Pet Expo 'to do list'.

As they sat at their desks, Belle picked up her list and spoke to Kelly, "We are so close to being ready for this expo. I'm actually proud of us."

"What's left to be done?" asked Kelly.

"The major job now is all the printing and putting the Information Packs together. Then closer to the date, we'll have all the last minute things to finish up," replied Belle, "Could you please get started with the printing and once it's done, I'll help with the packs?"

"Sure. I printed all the Sponsor's Brochures; Council Dog Parks and Dog Registration Rules a couple of weeks ago during all the commotion with Jane so all that's left is the Barking Guide and the New Owner's Guide."

"I thought Jane was complaining that there was no paper available for printing and copying?"

"She was complaining about it the morning she died. In fact, I think that was the last complaint I heard from her but when we came back on Thursday, the photocopy room was fully stocked and as we had some of the documents ready to do, I printed them for when the guides were ready."

"Well done," Belle praised, "Finish printing the guides and let me know when I can help."

Kelly started the printing while Belle gazed into space. She too was sure Jane had complained last week that there was no paper in the photocopier room.

If there was no paper on Tuesday morning when Jane complained and the room got sealed by the police on Tuesday afternoon, how was there paper in it when the police released the room on Thursday morning?

They must have received a paper delivery on Tuesday morning. Lucy didn't mention seeing Noah but Belle remembered Paige commenting about seeing Noah's van in the carpark.

Did anyone else mention seeing Noah? Belle opened up the spreadsheet holding all the information they had gathered. She smiled, they had been busy, there was a lot of data and they still needed to add the Harry information. Thankfully Jules was great at organising so the material was well categorised.

There was only one mention of Noah in the alibi section of the spreadsheet. Kevin had talked about his near miss with Paige at 11.45am outside of Mark's office and then the run in with Noah and his empty trolley at about 12.15pm on his way back from the bathroom.

Reading about trolley crashes triggered another memory for Belle. Lucy had mentioned something about Noah and Arthur nearly having an accident but she hadn't said when it was.

"Arthur, when did you nearly collide with Noah and the paper delivery?" Belle called out.

Belle was nearly sorry she'd asked as Arthur started ranting. In summary, Arthur had nearly crashed into Noah and his full trolley at the lift just before 12.00 noon that Tuesday when he was leaving the council offices to go to his church.

That explains the paper delivery. Noah had a full trolley when he saw Arthur and an empty trolley when he saw Kevin. But it doesn't explain why Noah didn't try and see Lucy; and why Noah failed to mention that he'd been here on the day of the murder.

Belle grabbed a pen and paper and started a timeline using the information detailed in the spreadsheet.

Paige's alibi had her in the carpark between 11.35am and 11.45am. If she saw Noah's van as she left the carpark, it gives Paige time to get upstairs and crash into Kevin at about 11.45am as he went to the bathroom.

Then if Noah loaded his trolley and entered the council offices, the timing was right for nearly running over Arthur at 11.55am.

This puts Paige safely back in the office and Kevin in the Men's Room from 11.55am to 12.15pm. Arthur was on his way to church and Frank had left earlier for his dance class so assuming Kelly and Jack were telling the truth and were at their desks, the corridors were empty for those twenty minutes.

Jane went to the bathroom around 11.30am according to Paige and if Jane was slacking off as normal, it would not be unusual for her to be gone for more than thirty minutes.

The timing was right for Jane to be coming back from the bathroom and running into Noah and taking him straight to the photocopier room to deliver the paper. That would explain how an outsider gained access to the secure room.

The only wild card was Lucy. Lucy was on her mail run from 11.30am until 12.00pm. A quick stop back at the office to pick up Mark's envelopes then off delivering those until 12.30pm. It would be close but not impossible. Jane and Noah could be in the photocopier room before Lucy returned at

12.00pm then Noah could leave after Lucy had started her envelope deliveries, running into Kevin with the empty trolley at 12.15pm.

The timings fit. And he knew the setup of the office. He even knew about the touchy photocopier and the 'Out of Order' sign. Noah definitely had opportunity.

What about motive? There was nothing in the spreadsheet because they hadn't even considered him as a suspect. Belle leant back in her chair and tried to remember all of Lucy's prattle after their first date. She remembered that Noah had an obsession about bullies. Maybe it was as simple as that, Jane started her normal bullying behaviour and Noah lost his temper? And Noah did seem to have a strange empathy with the murderer. Regardless, this was something the police could investigate.

Maybe Belle didn't have the 'why' fully identified but she was pretty sure she had the 'who' and the 'how'.

What did she do now? Should she contact Sgt Harris or maybe talk to Charlie first? Whatever she did, she needed to do it quickly because Lucy was bound to have plans with Noah soon, possibly even tonight. And she did not want her sister dating a murderer.

Belle picked up her mobile phone and ironically, walked into the empty photocopier room for some privacy for the phone call she was about to make. She looked around the room and dialled Charlie's number, "I know who killed Jane."

And every murder mystery has to have a murderer ...

A nd this murderer had just been identified.

"I know who did it," repeated Belle.

Charlie listened intently while Belle explained her thoughts.

"It all fits," replied Charlie, "Let me find Sgt Harris and I'll call you back. Can you wait where you are?"

Belle assented and hung up the phone. The minutes seem to drag on forever as Belle waited for the phone to ring. She looked around the photocopier room imagining Jane's last moments. Did she see it coming? Or was she too caught up in whatever vile notion was spewing from her mouth? Belle remembered Jennifer's comment about someone wanting to 'shut that mouth' and was positive that would be the reason Jane got hit over the head.

Belle looked at the reams of paper which had pointed her in the right direction. Without them, it was quite possible that Noah would have gotten away with it. Or maybe not, they might have expanded their suspect list to include him and notice the discrepancies in his story. It was a moot point now.

The phone finally rang and Sgt Harris said, "Thanks for your thoughts Belle. Could you please go over them again? And just to advise, this call is being recorded."

Belle reiterated her thoughts while Sgt Harris listened quietly, "I think we need to bring Mr. Bradley in to answer some questions."

"When do you think he will be contacted?" Belle asked, "He probably has a date with my sister tonight and I don't want her in any danger."

"I will do some checking here immediately and then contact him this afternoon. And I would like for you to keep this to yourself until then, we don't know how he will react and I don't want you in any danger," Sgt Harris said forcefully, "Can you do that?"

"Yes," Belle replied, "Lucy is at the dentist so she's out of harm's way for a couple of hours. Can somebody let me know what happens?"

"Officially, no, I can't tell you," replied Sgt Harris, "But unofficially, I'll make sure you know when it's safe."

Belle returned to the office and jumped every time her phone chirped. It was a long afternoon. She received a phone call from Charlie about 3.00pm.

"Noah Bradley was arrested this afternoon and officially charged with Jane King's murder," Charlie quietly informed Belle, "After being questioned, he confessed to the murder and actually seemed relieved that all the pretence is over."

"It's over?"

"For us, pretty much," replied Charlie, "We'll need you to come to the station tomorrow to make a statement but his confession has simplified everything."

"Can I tell everyone here?"

"Yes, it's public knowledge now. You can say he's been charged and that he confessed but keep your part quiet until we've taken your statement,"

"Can I tell Lucy?" Belle asked.

"Of course but keep it between you two."

The friends ended the call after making plans to meet the following day.

****

The following Sunday arrived with a burst of summer sun. The temperature was forecasted to be in the low thirties. Belle and Lucy had arranged a barbeque for their friends at their folk's house with Sam cooking. Everyone was interested in Monday's developments but with their Tuesday night dinner being cancelled, neither Lucy nor Belle had had the opportunity to share, hence a barbeque where everyone could hear at once.

For Belle, much of Tuesday had been spent at the Police Station going over her version of possible events. For Lucy, after Belle dropped the bombshell on Monday night, the rest of the week had been spent in disbelief, wondering how she could have been so blind; wavering between belief in

Noah's innocence and facing the reality that she had been dating a murderer.

The twins arrived early to help their parents set up. Aside from Laura, Sam, Belle and Lucy, the others coming were Georgie and Oliver, Jules and Andrew plus Charlie. Cooper had even wrangled an invitation and was looking forward to an afternoon filled with scraps. This was not a first for the Andersons, Belle and Lucy had been bringing their friends home for meals all through their schooling. Now the crowd just expanded to include current partners.

Sam's normal simple barbeque had been enhanced by Laura's need to provide a wider range of food plus include some healthy choices. As well as Sam's chops, sausages and chips, today's menu featured marinated minute steak portions, chicken skewers and some seasoned eggplant for the resident vegetarian, Georgie. Accompaniments were a choice of salads, fresh crunchy bread with a fruit platter and lemon tart to follow.

By 1.15pm everyone had arrived and was settled around the table with a drink. With the twin's help, Laura had all the salads and desserts ready for eating so had joined her guest for a pre-dinner drink. Sam was tending to the barbeque but was within earshot and eagerly listening to every word as Belle started to explain the events of the past two days.

"It started with the paper which apparently magically appeared in the photocopy room while the room was sealed by the police. Jane was complaining about the lack of paper on Tuesday morning but Kelly definitely did the printing two day later on Thursday so there must have been a delivery in between these times," explained Belle, "The police sealed the room on Tuesday after Jane was killed and released it on Thursday morning which only leaves Tuesday morning after Jane was complaining as a possible time for the delivery."

"If that's the case, why wasn't Noah included as a suspect when we put the list together?" asked Jules.

"I … umm we," Belle glanced at Lucy, "We didn't realise he'd been at the office that day. It wasn't until later that it became clear."

Belle continued, "Paige saw Noah's van in the carpark offices on Tuesday morning and both Kevin and Arthur placed Noah at the council offices on the same day with his delivery trolley; Arthur saw him with the full trolley and Kevin with the empty trolley. This says what time Noah was in the photocopier room."

"But how did he get the paper into the photocopier room? Didn't you say it was a secure room?" asked Laura as she handed some snacks around.

"I thought about that and the only answer which made sense was that Jane let him in. Certainly no-one else mentioned letting him into the photocopier room."

"But why did he kill her?" asked Georgie.

"From what Sgt Harris let slip, Jane was ridiculing Noah's chances of staying with Lucy. Noah just lost control and picked up the nearby stapler and hit her," replied Belle, "Jennifer's comment about someone wanting to shut Jane's mouth was exactly what happened."

"I think it was a bit more complicated than that," Charlie interjected, "It seems his childhood was less than idyllic. His Dad was quite abusive, both verbally and physically and when Jane aimed her vitriol at him, Noah was reminded of previous days."

"What happened when the police questioned him?" asked Oliver.

"I wasn't there," replied Charlie, "But I heard he just collapsed and confessed. Which was lucky because we had no forensic evidence against him. Our only evidence was circumstantial."

"Why do you think he did it?" Lucy asked quietly.

"Luce, I think it was a spur of the moment action. The stapler was there, he picked it up and thumped her," said Charlie, "I don't think he planned it and I'm sure his lawyers will argue manslaughter rather than murder."

Lucy nodded.

"But," Charlie continued, "When she didn't get up, he was thinking enough to not panic. To wipe his fingerprints from the stapler, to turn off the lights, to use his jumper as a glove when putting up the 'Out of Order' sign and then leave. It was just bad luck when he ran into Arthur and Kevin that day and more bad luck when Paige saw his van in the carpark."

"When he confessed, did Noah give any explanation?" asked Belle.

"He believes Jane deserved to die," Charlie sighed, "He believes people who are so self-centred that they forget others have feelings don't have the right to live. Especially when these people judge others and spout their opinions about things that are none of their business."

"That does tie in with what he said about not accepting being treated with disrespect. Perhaps he was trying to justify what he'd done," mused Belle.

"Is this all my fault?" Lucy asked quietly.

Everyone around the table was quick to negate this idea.

"Lucy, Noah was on the edge," insisted Charlie, "If he hadn't killed Jane, it would have been someone else who said the wrong thing to him. Jane died because she unfortunately mouthed off to the wrong person at the wrong time. It was Noah's choice and his actions. It's not right and it's not Jane's fault but it's definitely not your fault."

Lucy nodded, "It's a pity that all the resources Noah had about bullying didn't help him when dealing with his own bully."

She picked up some empty plates and carried them inside.

As Belle watched Lucy go inside she thought to herself, 'who could have imagined that Lucy's love life would inadvertently result in fatal consequences.'

Happily ever after ...

S everal weeks had passed.
The office had returned to a new normal.

Mark's wakeup call had not lasted long. His empathetic, vulnerable side had vanished as if it had never appeared. Back to wheeling and dealing, always chasing the money and not realising what he was losing in the meantime. Mark and Alex Petras had vowed to behave themselves in the future and Jennifer was choosing to believe them.

Jennifer had finally forgiven Lucy for the repeated murderer accusations and they spoke most weeks as Jennifer completed her executor duties and handled all the small details that are required when a life ends. As promised, Lucy passed on all the discoveries they found during the investigation and often spoke about Jane at work, both good and bad.

Arthur on the other hand was slowly moving towards the current century. After seeing the positive side to police work, his wife had finally stood her ground and said she would be supporting their daughter's dream of joining the force and if he wouldn't, then maybe they needed to have a larger discussion. The thought of losing his beloved wife was more than Arthur could bear so for now he was unenthusiastically keeping his opinion to himself. Whether this would translate to an easier work colleague, they would have to wait and see.

Kevin had reverted to his pre-murder self, searching out auction novelties, online chatting with strangers around the world and arguing sports with Frank. And if he ever felt a fleeting longing for red velvet cupcakes and their provider, he kept it to himself.

And Frank's attempt to woo his wife had been successful. Their anniversary had been a triumph and she was so touch by his efforts with the dance classes, they had even booked a European cruise for next year. No-one ever discovered his secret and he looked years younger, so the mystery remained.

Frank was also keeping in touch with Harry. They decided to catch up monthly to watch a game or the races on a Saturday afternoon. Harry was now missing both Mary and Jane but having Frank around gave him someone else to talk to who also hadn't heard all of his stories.

Harry and Jennifer had discussed Jane's last wishes and were planning on donating much of the money to charities they felt Jane would have liked. Harry was going to take some of the money and travel to Las Vegas as he and Jane had planned. He was trying to talk Frank into coming with him.

Unlike Mark, Paige had taken her second chance seriously. Being the chief suspect, if only for a short while, had scared her silly and taught Paige the concept of consequences. As an office colleague, she had dramatically improved and was shadowing Belle as a role model rather than Frank and Kevin. In her personal life, she had come to some hard realisations. It hadn't been easy but Paige and Lucy had been spending time together at the gym and it seemed to be helping both of them.

Kelly was still Kelly. Unflappable and a wonderful helper and friend for Belle, although she kept forgetting to change her privacy settings on Instagram and Facebook much to Belle's annoyance.

Today was the Pet Expo. The culmination of Belle and the team's work for the last few months.

As the people crowded into the Civic Park waiting for the expo to be officially opened by the mayor, Belle, Lucy and Jack looked over the park from their vantage point near the stage. There were smiles all around them. The exhibitors had arrived and were busy setting up. The band was sounding good and the decorations brightened the park. The chefs were creating interesting smells from the tents and the doggie taste testers were ready to go. Everything seemed on schedule.

Across the park they saw Georgie having a wonderful time trying to hold a border collie puppy who wanted to investigate those good smells emanating from the different tents and food vans. Georgie looked up and waved to her friends. Tuesday night dinners had been exciting at first, buoyed with solving the murder then subdued at the result but as Lucy returned to normal, so did the get togethers. Jules, Drew and her future mother-in-law had reached an agreement about the wedding venue; it would be at the zoo. Jules was quietly cheering. With Lucy spending more time in the gym getting fit with Paige, Charlie was trying to convince her to run a half marathon, having given up on persuading Georgie. Everyone should have such a great group of friends.

Lucy had taken Noah's behaviour badly. How could he think killing Jane was what she wanted? That she would be pleased? He obviously didn't know her. And how could she have missed the signs? But these events had given her the push to make a change. She had taken Jane's old job while planning her next move. The last month had shown Lucy how many people hid their terrors from the world and she'd decided she wanted to play a part in helping folks face those demons. Finding a part time job and enrolling in a Bachelor of Social Work was her first step down this path.

Belle was just glad the puzzle had been solved. Lucy was safe and the Pet Expo was a success. Jack was talking about moving to another area to forward his political ambitions and Belle was secretly planning to take over his job. She had lots of ideas and couldn't wait to implement them. Council pet owners didn't know what was coming.

As the trio headed to the food tents to get a drink, Jack casually dropped his arm around Belle's shoulder. She looked up to his kind, cautious face, leant into the hug and smiled. She turned to Lucy, "I'm glad the last few months are over. Hey what was that surprise you were going to give the office?

Lucy laughed, "I wanted to organise an event that would improve the morale within the office. There is a company here in Adelaide that offers to recreate 'the Vegas experience without the airfare'. They hire out quality casino tables including blackjack, roulette, poker, big wheel and craps plus provide the dealers. I thought a Casino Night was a bit different and would give us all the chance to relax and reset and make the office a happier place to come every day."

"That sounds like fun," replied Belle.

"And I didn't even know how much Jane would have liked it. Funny how things work out," Lucy reflected, "Trivial decisions and their consequences can be surprising."

The End

Author Bio

"*Consequences can be fatal*" is the first novel for Lee Smith.

With a background in Business and years of teaching in front of an adult classroom, Lee has seen many different faces of humanity and understands the ins and outs of office politics. She creates her mysteries in beautiful Adelaide, South Australia, surrounded by her own beloved Ridgebacks, Cooper and Scout.

www.ingramcontent.com/pod-product-compliance
Lightning Source LLC
Chambersburg PA
CBHW071717140626
46557CB00012B/912